Dale Mayer

MAN
DOWN
GIDEON

GIDEON: MAN DOWN, BOOK 3
Beverly Dale Mayer
Valley Publishing Ltd.

ISBN-13: 978-1-778863-30-1
Print Edition

Books in This Series:

About This Book

There is no greater motive than bloodlust, DNA, and revenge mixed up in a cocktail of hatred ...

Gideon immediately returned to Coronado base at the call for help. After hearing the issues facing him, he dove right in, knowing that he could bury the pain of his past broken relationship the same as he always had. The fact that they'd lived here in this city years ago didn't make it harder. Yet, once he caught sight of Pearl, it made it almost impossible.

Pearl broke up their relationship years ago, only to realize almost immediately that she'd made a major mistake. She quickly returned to Coronado, only to find that Gideon had shipped out overseas. Now still working at the same place as before, Pearl sees him in the stairwell, and the shock hits her hard, both with hope and dread. When she returns home that evening to something completely unbelievable happening before her eyes, Gideon is the first person she turns to.

Gideon doesn't know how Pearl ends in the middle of his case, but she is, and she's not moving any time soon. Now if only he could trust that she would stay this time ...

Sign up to be notified of all Dale's releases here!
https://geni.us/DaleNews

PROLOGUE

J ASPER WATCHED AS Elizabeth and Masters walked out,
holding hands. Jasper was happy for them, he was.
Neither of them had had any expectation of finding a
partner in this lifetime, but it seemed that sometimes things
happened, even when it was least expected. Jasper was happy
for his friend. As he sat, contemplating whether Gideon was
the next person to call or not, his phone rang. He smiled to
see Gideon's name on the screen. "How did you know I was
just gonna call you?"

"Because, when shit hits the fan, it's usually me you guys
call," he replied succinctly. "How bad do you need me? On
the red eye, or will tomorrow do?"

"How about yesterday?"

"Shit, I figured you would say that. You want to get me
caught up?"

"I'll send you some details. Where are you flying in
from?"

"Don't worry about it," he replied. "I promise I'll be
ready, in working order, when I get there."

"You'll need to be. We just found our navy investigator,
the one we thought was dead and gone. Meanwhile he'd
been held and tortured for the last four months."

"One of our own?" Gideon asked in a shocked tone.

"Yeah. One who had been here as part of the military's investigation team, yet was more or less written off."

"Crap. Will he make it?"

"He'll live, but it'll be a long, slow road to recovery."

"Jeez. I'm there. I'm there. That shit never goes down well in my world."

"No, it sure doesn't for us either," Jasper noted, "but we still have a few good people here to find out what the hell's going on."

"Yeah, well, I'm worried about Mason."

"You and me both," Jasper said. "He's holding his own in the hospital, but we're getting jack shit trying to get an investigation going."

"That's all right. I got that nailed."

"Yeah, you say that," Jasper replied, "and you're joking about it, but nobody here is joking. So keep that in mind when you get here. So far, we haven't found anything. No sign of the sniper, no sign of anything, and this other shit keeps happening."

"And you don't know that this other deal, that *whatever else is going on*, had nothing to do with it?"

"I suspect it did, but we're still turning over rocks, trying to get answers."

"That's good to hear," Gideon said. "You know me. I'm one of the best rock-turners in the business. I'll see you in the morning." And, with that, he disconnected.

CHAPTER 1

G IDEON WARRICK STEPPED off the plane, hoisted his backpack, and walked several steps forward, realizing he was almost in the exact same position Mason would have been when he'd been shot. Gideon glanced around, assessing the shooting capabilities of anybody who would take him out. Was the injury a mistake or just a bad shot that didn't kill Mason? Was it deliberate? Was somebody just warning him? Were they warning somebody else? Maybe they were playing the long game, like do this or else.

Gideon looked around, but nobody seemed to care or notice that he was here. He half smiled at that. He was usually pretty good at blending into the crowd. Another dozen guys got off the transporter with him. He moved over to the side, waiting to see whether anybody interrupted him or questioned his movements. ... Nobody did.

Shaking his head at that, he kept walking until somebody stepped directly in his path. Surprised, and yet happy to think somebody might be challenging his movements. *Jasper.* Gideon reached out for a handshake. "Hey, I wasn't sure whether you got my messages or not."

"Got them," Jasper confirmed, "and we're heading straight to the hospital."

"Why? Is Mason worse?" he asked, concern in his tone.

"No, but there's a chance that Nicholas is able to speak."

"Nicholas, as in …" Gideon frowned, as he tried to recall what Masters had told him, then remembered, "Ah, the investigator who was held captive?"

"Exactly. His sister is also at the hospital. She's under guard with Nicholas, Tesla, and Mason."

"Sounds like I'll get to meet the whole family."

"You will, and you also get to meet Masters."

"I already know Masters." Gideon shook his head. "I've worked with him a couple times."

"You okay with him?"

"Absolutely. He was good to work with and stayed out of my way," he noted, as if that meant more to him than anything else. "That's as important as anything else."

Jasper laughed. "That is so you." Then he slapped him on the shoulder and added, "Let's go."

As Jasper headed over to a small car, Gideon snorted. "What the hell is up with the tiny car?"

"It blends in a little easier."

"Ah, good point."

"I do have a truck assigned to you."

"Thanks. I was just wondering whether anybody was keeping track of my movements or has been completely oblivious as to who came and went off this base."

"Whoever is coming and going here should already have clearance," Jasper pointed out. "Yet I understand what you're saying. Nobody is stopping you or checking your credentials. Correct. Though you are on camera, of course."

"Sure, but—"

"That's among quite a few recommendations I'll be making for future safety of our personnel after this," Jasper grumbled. "The fact of the matter is, what happened to Mason shouldn't have happened, but it did, which usually means that somebody on the inside gave away some top secret intel."

"I'm not sure any top secret intel was involved to give away," Gideon countered. "It was a simple open-and-shut case. A sniper and his target. What we need is the motive."

"What we can't find is the sniper."

"You'll find him all right," Gideon replied. "Did you check for John Does in the hospital?"

Jasper turned and stared at him.

"If I hired a sniper, you could bet that he wouldn't live five minutes after his kill shot, and he couldn't be ID'd either. I would cut off his fingers and his toes, take out his eyeballs and teeth, the whole works," he explained, with a bark of a laugh. "And if anybody out there is as serious as I suspect they are, they would do the same thing—unless of course the sniper was the mastermind behind it all."

"Your version sounds too professional for me," Jasper noted, with a headshake. "Which is why I'm on this side of the line, thinking Mason's attack was some novice at work."

"I hate to say it, but, to me, it sounded like drugs were involved, but addictions are everywhere these days. Every base in the world has a drug problem to some degree," he said. "Hell, every town does too. However, this is pretty big deal for it to be"—he winced—"*just* drugs."

"And that's a whole other discussion," Jasper stated. Then he smiled. "It's good to have you around, man."

"You just want somebody to bounce ideas off of?"

"I sure do. Plus, you know Mason."

"I sure do, and that's another reason I'm here. Mason and I go way back."

"Seems like Mason goes way back with half the world." Jasper sighed. "We've had plenty of volunteers asking for guard duty, off the payroll, so that everybody can get in and do something to help out."

"You shouldn't turn that down," Gideon replied in a serious tone. "As long as you've got men you can clear, that you're certain aren't part of this, that we can trust, then you should take them up on it."

"I've got a roster going, and Tesla is working with it as well. At first, she was against any guard, but we've talked her into it now."

"She never did like being corralled, did she?"

Jasper laughed. "She hasn't changed."

"Good. She's one hell of a woman. She and Mason are the only couple out there who've ever made me rethink the whole marriage thing. I never thought it would have worked in our line of work, probably because I've seen more marriages destroyed on these bases than people coming together in any good and lasting way."

"You and me both," Jasper agreed. "I've got to tell you though, I found somebody too. So did Masters."

Gideon stared at Jasper as if he had sprouted horns or something. "Seriously?" Gideon scoffed. "Is that Mason's luck spreading to all his men once again? What were they called... the Keepers or something?"

"I don't know," Jasper admitted, with a grin. "That's a legendary joke, but I don't think anybody is laughing right now."

"Maybe not, but it sounds like there's still some influence, joke or not."

"The Keepers are real, alive and kicking," Jasper said, "although I haven't heard too much of them lately. It's one of those things where people are teased about finding love, but nobody ever has a serious conversation about it. Still, all the men in Mason's group seem to wind up happily married. So, prior to this, I would have laughed if anybody had predicted that I would find somebody myself. Yet I did, so it is what it is."

"Good enough. So, how did you meet her?"

He winced. "She was an ER nurse at the hospital here, when Mason got shot. I made the mistake of telling her that, if she saw anything suspicious, to let me know. However, instead of letting me know, she thought she'd go one better and videotaped somebody."

"Oh, crap."

"Yeah, *Oh, crap* is right. Anyway, she's under guard herself now and laying low, staying out of trouble until we can get this solved."

"So, that's your Keepers story, but you mentioned that Masters found somebody too?"

"He did. *Elizabeth*. She's the sister of the investigator who was held captive."

"Wow." Gideon dropped his head as he laughed. "So all I need to do is find somebody in trouble and enlist the help of other people, is that it?"

"That might work for you," Jasper said, with a laugh, "but I wouldn't count on it. We've had a lot of people involved, though I can't say any marriages have come out of this yet."

"Yeah, I hear you there." Gideon waved his hands. "It figures all the luck would run out just before I got here."

"Oh, I don't know about that, but I don't particularly know of any prospects who'll be in the picture for you this time."

"You never know," Gideon noted casually.

As they pulled into the parking lot of the hospital, Gideon looked up and sighed. "The one person I was ever close to worked right here, but she up and moved back East before I could formalize the relationship. I always figured that she ran before I could ask. That she knew I was gonna pop the question, and she ran instead."

Jasper stopped on the sidewalk. "Seriously?"

He nodded. "She was a physiotherapist, but she'd done her five years and was itching to relocate. I'm a military lifer," he said, with half a smile. "Still, I figured we could work it out. It's not as if she couldn't work in town, going private or whatever. It just didn't work out," he muttered, with a shrug.

"I doubt that she's here."

"No, she isn't. … She went back East."

Jasper didn't say anything. "What was her name?"

"Pearl, Pearl Laverne." He laughed. "She hated her name growing up, but it was her grandmother's name—a very good old-fashioned name, according to her mother."

"Sounds like it. I like it though. Is she tall, with black hair?" Jasper had a smirk on his face.

At that, Gideon stopped and asked suspiciously, "She is. Why?"

"I thought I saw somebody with that name tag, and that's an odd name, so it stuck," he shared. "Yet I've seen so many people around here, and I'm looking so much more closely now because we can't afford to take any chances. I just thought that her face was striking, as well as her name, which stood out."

"I doubt that it's her," Gideon snapped, a bit harsher than he intended.

"You got a picture of her?"

Frowning, Gideon grabbed his phone and swiped through his photo gallery.

"What?" Jasper asked. "I figured you carried a photo in your wallet."

Gideon shrugged. "I did, until I lost my wallet and that picture." He clicked on the last photo he had of her. He held it up for Jasper to have a good look. "See? I told you that you couldn't have seen her."

Jasper looked at it and whistled. "That *is* her."

"No way, she was dying to get out, man." He shook his head, but, inside, hope and dread warred for supremacy in his heart. "She wouldn't have come back."

"Unless she thought you would be here."

"I went off and did a bunch of missions as far overseas as I could get at that point in time," he shared, with a wry smile. "Not exactly the easy way to mend a broken heart, but it worked, more or less."

"I wonder if it worked though," Jasper countered, "or whether you're still open to her."

"I'm not open to anything in that direction. I never go backward."

"Maybe not, but I'm not sure she even went forward."

"That's her problem," Gideon stated briskly. "What's over and done with is over and done."

As they stepped into the hospital, Jasper led the way to Mason's room. As they took the stairs up to the second floor, the door to the second floor opened, and a woman stepped into the stairwell. As she passed them, Jasper lightly punched Gideon, who was checking the stairs below them. Gideon looked up, took one look at her, his gaze brushing past, only to come swinging back to her again. He sucked in his breath.

The woman gave them a polite blank look, then she froze.

"Jeez," Gideon whispered.

One of her eyebrows slowly rose. "Gideon?" she asked softly.

He nodded, otherwise frozen, wondering how the hell fate would have done this to him.

She looked over at Jasper, back at Gideon, and her smile fell away. "Nice to see you," she replied formally. With that, she picked up her gaze and raced down the stairs gracefully, leaving Gideon standing there, dumbfounded, as he stared after her.

PEARL RACED TO the bottom of the stairs, appearing calm, but, once out of his sight, she ran all the way down to the basement level, her breathing harsh, her face flushed. She'd finally come face-to-face with the man she'd returned to Coronado for—only to find out that he was long gone, having left soon after she had. Since then, every time she turned around, it seemed as if he was here, only to find out he wasn't. Now that he was truly here, what did she do? … Like an idiot, she ran as far and as fast as she could. Now she was huddled in the basement, desperate to reenact those last few minutes all over again.

She closed her eyes and wrapped her arms tightly around her chest, as she tried to control her breathing.

The stupidest thing she'd ever done was to walk away from him five years ago, and now, when finally given an opportunity to rectify her mistake, he'd stared at her blankly, as if she wasn't even there. It had broken her heart. Yet she realized that he might have been just as shocked as she was. He didn't even know she was in town, whereas she felt like she'd been looking for him forever. That was so typical of the way her world went these days, as if nothing was in sync. It hadn't been ever since she'd walked away five years ago.

It hadn't taken her long to realize it was the biggest mistake of her life. She'd heard he'd gone back overseas into the war zones, and she wondered if she had pushed him there, as he headed into some of the most dangerous areas possible. He was an investigator, a hell of a good one, but he'd often told her that the only good investigators were the ones who understood how things worked out in the real world. Therefore, as long as he hid away behind a desk, he couldn't understand what these men were going through.

When she and Gideon were together, she had pleaded with him to not go back out on these missions. She couldn't face losing him. Yet, when push had come to shove, ... *she'd* been the one to walk away—not sure that she was ready for the commitment, not sure that she was ready for whatever it would take to keep him at home. Even if she kept him at home, surely he would hold it against her, especially if he wasn't ready to set down roots. She knew she wasn't ready, but, damn it, watching him go off to war wasn't her thing.

When her time was up here, five years ago, and an opportunity had come for her to transfer, she'd taken it, barely giving him any notice. She'd just run. She sold off her furniture, not having that much to begin with, and had raced back East. It had been a good thing in terms of her career, as she'd picked up new training opportunities. However, as far as her heart went, it had been brutal. It had been so very depressing because it was not at all the way she'd thought it would be. Not having him in her life had left a huge void that she hadn't expected, didn't want, and would now do anything to fill. Yet, seeing him just now, what had she done to fill that void?

Absolutely nothing.

She had accomplished nothing, leaving behind the one good thing in her life. Again. She couldn't even get her voice to work properly and had bolted, just like the scared rabbit she was. Maybe she'd done it once, but now she felt as if she was doing it all over again. She gave herself another few minutes and a hard talking to, then pushed herself back out in the direction she'd intended to go in the first place.

As she walked up to the main floor and entered the chaos in ER, one of the nurses walked over and handed her the material she had come to get.

"Thanks for picking it up."

She smiled at her. "No problem."

"Are you okay? You look like you just saw a ghost."

"Yeah, I did." She shook her head. "Somebody I used to know."

"Oh, everybody transfers out, then, for whatever reason, it seems they can't get enough, and they all come back," the nurse replied, with a knowing smile. "Stick around long enough and it's almost as if we recycle them." With half a laugh at her own joke, the nurse headed back into her department.

Pearl stood here, staring down at the material she'd come to collect, wondering at just how pathetic her words had sounded. As soon as she realized she'd made a mistake—which was basically immediately, some five years ago—she should have come back, like a homing pigeon. But, unlike a homing pigeon, she returned just to find out her home was no longer here, as Gideon was gone.

CHAPTER 2

PEARL WALKED BACK upstairs, looking for Gideon around every corner. When she didn't see him, she calmed down once again and headed over to the Physiotherapy Department and to her patients. She wished the hospital had better services for some of these people. What they needed was a specialized facility, and she'd seen and worked at a couple of them. Some were unbelievable at what they could offer a patient, but here? It was more a case of what worked for one was supposed to work for everybody. Thus the physiotherapist had to adapt what they had to work for everyone.

Similar to the way the public school system that worked to move a lot of people through the essential process, but, for those students who needed a little something extra, it wasn't the best system. She'd found that with rehab too. It worked very well for a lot of people, but for many who needed a little bit more, a little bit extra, it was not the ideal situation.

She'd certainly heard about other clinics and other facilities where more specialized services were available. She walked into her office to find her coworker John standing there, waiting for her. She gave him a quick frown. "What's the matter?"

"Hey." He gave her a shrug. "Just wondering what took you so long."

Her eyebrows shut up. "What's the matter?" she asked, with a harsh tone. "Are you checking up on me now?"

His gaze was a little more guarded as he replied, "Maybe. For all I know, you're hanging out in stairwells."

She frowned at him, not sure where that was coming from or why he would even attempt such a remark. "If you've got a problem, then say so."

"It's not that I've got a problem," he noted, "but other people might."

"I don't know what you're talking about. I've never had an issue with anybody here," she exclaimed.

"I'm not saying you're having an issue now. It's just that, ... while you were gone, some people talked."

She stared at him. "When you say *some talked*, what do you mean? What talk?"

He winced. "That one little bird has a tendency to talk about you."

Pearl flushed with anger because Betty, a woman who worked in the front offices, did seem to have it in for Pearl. She didn't know why or what she'd ever done to her, but, no doubt, if trouble was brewing, it was coming from her. "I see," Pearl said softly, "and of course you didn't back me up."

"Remember that it's a dog-eat-dog world up here," he told her, raising his hands in defense, "I don't back up anybody, and I don't expect anybody to back me up."

"Got it." She gave him a curt nod. "Thanks for the heads-up at least."

"Hey, I'm just telling you that rumors are flying around."

"Yet she has no business spreading rumors of any kind," Pearl declared stiffly.

Once in her office, she closed the door, not sure what she was even supposed to do about this. Betty took every opportunity to make snide remarks and innuendos when Pearl wasn't around. It wasn't exactly a good working environment, and she'd only been hanging on because she didn't know what else to do right now. She'd pretty much made the decision that it was time to just leave and see if she could start again somewhere else, but then she found Gideon in the stairway.

She sat here for a long moment to get her head wrapped around what she'd seen, when a knock came on her door and her boss walked in. Pearl waited.

Maria smiled at her. "I see you've already heard."

"John doesn't miss an opportunity," she shared lightly. "He won't back anybody up, but he's pretty quick to throw us to the wolves." Pearl shrugged away the unpleasantness.

"I will tell you that your person of interest was caught gossiping about you and that she has been reprimanded for it."

Surprised, Pearl frowned. "I just now walked in and heard she was talking about me."

"Ah, I should have figured that's what John was doing, as soon as you headed here." Maria turned around to glare out at the main offices through the glass door. "If he won't help the situation, spreading the gossip makes it worse."

"It absolutely does," Pearl agreed, "but you and I both know that he's a damn good therapist."

Maria nodded. "That's part of the problem. We tolerate a lot from everybody because we're short-staffed and because we need all the gifted people we can get. I just wish the gifted people didn't come with big issues."

"They don't *all* come with big issues," Pearl pointed out, with a laugh.

Maria added, "Yet you seem to have collected more than your fair share of them in your department."

"Sadly, I can only agree with that," Pearl muttered, with an eye roll.

"Anyway, just to let you know before you have to deal with it yourself, I dealt with it."

"How long before she quits?" she muttered.

"Not soon enough, unless we want to make a big issue out of it, but we can't do anything to speed that process along."

"*Right.*"

"Tolerate it the best you can, and hopefully, with this reprimand, Betty will be a little more circumspect in her blatant disregard for good manners."

"Not just good manners, it's basic professional etiquette to not pass around shit verbally that'll damage our relationship with our patients," she noted in frustration.

"I did tell her that. She just gave me that smirk, as if to say I didn't know what I was talking about."

"That always goes over well." Pearl had to laugh at that. "She's got that part down pat, doesn't she?"

"It's pretty damn irritating too," Maria muttered. "I've tried to get rid of her several times in the past, all with no luck. So, until she does something more egregious or bad enough that I can finally get other people onboard to remove her, just watch your *P*s and *Q*s."

"No need for *me* to watch my *P*s and *Q*s," Pearl quipped, "not with plenty of other people around here doing it for me. *I* don't like to gossip."

"Anyway, did you get that material downstairs?"

"And back again, yes, I did," she confirmed. She felt her face grow hot, as her mind flashed back to Gideon, clear as day.

"You look a little rattled."

"Yeah, I am in a way. I saw somebody in the stairwell that I hadn't seen in many years," she shared, "so that was a shock."

"Are you okay? Was it a good visit?"

"Sure." She waved her hand. "I'm fine. Besides, even if I wasn't and took the tiniest bit of time off, Miss Busybody would tell everyone it was an unexplained pregnancy from seventeen guys, all created in the last fortnight."

Her boss went off with a burst of laughter. "Oh my, hard to imagine how that would work, but you're right. Betty probably would."

"It just blows me away that somebody could be so mean and uncaring as to just make up all this shit," Pearl muttered. "Professionally speaking, it's absolutely stupefying that she has all this vitriol for me. What did I ever do to her?"

"She's not a physiotherapist, which I feel is the problem. She's not one of us. She's in an administrative role, and I think, in her mind, that's almost a diss. Maybe she feels inadequate for the job."

"With all her bullshit, she's made that *her* reality here, not about her job performance, and everybody already knows it," Pearl shared. "I get that you're keeping her because you don't want to rock the boat, but ..."

Maria explained calmly, "I've submitted a request for termination several times, but my boss always overrules me."

At that, Pearl frowned and asked, "Is anything going on there that we should know about?"

Maria stared at Pearl and then chuckled. "I wish there were because that would be a good way to deal with it and to finally make it all go away."

"But would it though?" Pearl asked. "How do these problematic people always end up smelling like a rose, while the rest of us are in the shitter, digging out of the crap?"

Her boss left, still chuckling over that one.

Although it was funny, it wasn't funny at all when you had somebody so obviously hating on you and doing everything they could to give you a bad rep. It made for a most unprofessional and difficult environment to work in. It had gotten so bad that several people had quit. Other people just tuned out the gossip gal, rather than get involved in that ugliness. Still, a certain number of people always wanted to hear any bit of juicy gossip, even if it wasn't true. The fact that it wasn't true drove Pearl even crazier when she thought about it.

But she had other things to deal with right now, other things to keep in mind, and one of those was Gideon. She was still completely stunned to see that he was here in town. That didn't mean he would be staying in town, of course. Yet, for the moment, he was in the building somewhere, and it brought almost a giddy feeling to her soul.

So many things in her life she would quickly or cheerfully ignore—including Betty the biddy from out in the main office. However, if it meant that Pearl had a chance of reconciling with Gideon, she wouldn't let anybody here have the slightest indication of that. Surely Betty would no doubt throw a spanner in the works immediately, just to spite her.

If Gideon walked in Betty's line of sight, Pearl had no doubt he would be subjected to some of the most horrific lies this woman could dream up. The fact that Betty still worked here was inexcusable, yet somehow she was. Even Maria, Pearl's direct boss, didn't have a clue why or how, much less how long it would be before Betty turned in her own notice and walked.

GIDEON PARTED WAYS with Jasper, who went to see Tesla and Mason. Gideon walked into Nicholas's hospital room and stopped when he realized the injured man was awake and talking with a woman. Both looked over at him.

The woman smiled, then jumped up to greet him. "Hi, my name is Elizabeth. Nicholas is my brother. While I'm so glad to see my brother is awake, he's not feeling all that great."

Gideon walked to the hospital bed with a smile, carefully shook the injured man's hand, and said, "So glad to see you, Nicholas. While you may not be fully awake and up walking around, we're damn glad to find you as well as you are."

"I'm pretty glad to be alive."

Gideon noted that Nicholas spoke somewhat slowly, yet clearly, without faltering. Still, he was holding back the pain, refusing to show it or trying not to. Gideon stood here for a long moment, studying the patient. Per his file, Nicholas was younger than he appeared, looking as if he'd been to hell and back. Captivity and torture would do that.

Then Nicholas spoke again. "I can't add much to the investigation of my own kidnapping and captivity. My captors never spoke in front of me. Never asked me any questions. But my gut tells me that I was taken as a *just in case, a backup plan.* Whatever their original plan was, it must have been blowing up, making them nervous. So they took me as added insurance."

"You want to explain that?" Jasper asked.

"My captors seemed to be middlemen, not part of the execution of the main plan, just hired to keep me hidden. Other than these impressions, I don't have a whole lot to tell you." Nicholas frowned, a confused and disoriented expression on his face. "If I knew more, I would give it to you, but I haven't had a whole lot of clarity in my world. I was kept drugged and isolated for a lot of my captivity. So the only thing I ever got to see was the one jailer who took way-too-much delight in pounding my face and body into the ground."

"That guy is dead," Elizabeth noted. She looked over at Gideon.

Gideon smiled at her. "I'm Gideon, and I'm here to help with the case."

She studied him for a long moment and then nodded. "Something about you guys is different." He cocked his head and waited. She shrugged. "It's hard to explain, but I get a sense of enhanced capability, indomitable spirit, that you won't allow this to beat you." She turned back to her brother and smiled. "Nicholas has that same look."

"I might have had it at one time," he clarified, "but things have changed in my world."

She whispered, "And you're not going back to work anytime soon."

His lips twitched. "They sure as hell better be paying me for all this," he muttered.

She snorted at that. "Considering that you were gone for months, I eventually had to go digging around for money to pay your house bills and whatnot. I'm sorry."

He rolled his eyes at that. "You found my stash, did

you?" he asked in a teasing tone.

"I found your investment documents," she admitted, "so we had to wonder if that was part of the reason you were kidnapped."

Nicholas looked over at Gideon. "If I'd come across that amount of money, I would have been thinking along those lines too," he shared carefully. "However, as far as I know, it had nothing to do with it."

"How so?"

"Nobody but my financial advisor, my good friend, and I know about the money. Most of it came from financial investments, but the original seed money came from a good friend of mine I helped with a startup. When it went big, he bought up my shares, and I ended up with something like thirty-two million," he shared, with a smirk.

Gideon nodded. "That's a lot of money."

"Yeah, it is, and both he and I were surprised. For the two of us, it was something too good to be true, but he did so well with his business that it was truly mind-boggling. He made good on the promises he made to me, but he also wanted to own the business all himself, so I sold him back my shares, then just invested the rest." He shrugged. "It's not as if I needed it, and my sister didn't either. So I figured, if she ever did need help, it was there. Of course I hadn't told her about it, so finding it must have been a bit of a shock."

"It was one hell of a shock," she replied, "as was the USB key."

He stared at her blankly. "What key?"

At that, Gideon stepped forward. "That USB key appears to have some damaging information on a case involving a young man called Gary Trojan, who went to prison, then died in prison, wrongfully convicted, according to your notes."

Nicholas stared at him, then slowly nodded. "Yes, I vaguely remember that now." He shifted painfully in his bed and then winced. "God." He rubbed his forehead. "The docs tell me my memory will slowly come back in pieces and parts, but I want it all to come back now."

"Of course," Gideon agreed, with a smile. "That's pretty normal too, but, in the meantime, we need you to try not to push it. The information will come in its own time."

"Yeah. people keep telling me that." Nicholas growled, looked over at his sister, about to say something, when an odd look came over his face. "I don't feel so good." He collapsed against the pillow, and instantly the machine at his side went off, sending out alarms everywhere. Everybody jumped out of the way, as the crash team flew in. Then the visitors were sent out into the hallway. Gideon held Elizabeth, who was shaking as she tried to peer in through the window.

"My God, Nicholas," she cried out.

"It's all right," Gideon replied, comforting her. "Let the doctors work."

She turned teary eyes to him. "But he seemed so fine."

"He was fine, right up until he wasn't," Gideon explained, with a soothing tone, "and that's how recovery happens. It appears as if everything is okay. Then it needs a little bit longer before he can pull it together. Give him that chance."

She nodded, but the tears were rolling down her face as she stared in the window of the door to Nicholas's hospital room.

Feeling helpless and not at all sure what he could do, Gideon tried to pull her attention away from the room and asked, "Did he say anything about who held him and why?"

She looked up at him, but her mind was clearly somewhere else. "He only saw the one man and couldn't identify him. As he already told you, just one guy who seemed to delight in beating the crap out of him for some reason. Beating on people must have been that gang's thing because two hooded gunmen showed up unannounced at my place, holding me captive, and one hit me multiple times. Thankfully Masters turned up when he did. That man ended up dying in my house, shot by his own partner."

"Your house? That's on record?"

"I guess so, and, if you ask me, good riddance. He was a bastard who just beat up on people, particularly women," she shared, staring off for a moment. "Or maybe he just enjoyed that more." She wiped her tears, looked back through the window, and turned to face Gideon. "If you're here to help, I hope you can get to the bottom of this and fast. Nicholas has been through enough, and it's not fair that he has to go through another health event like this again."

"The doctors are doing everything they can," Gideon stated, trying to keep her attention away from what they were doing in Nicholas's room, but her gaze was locked on the window.

Finally she turned, her shoulders slumped, and whispered, "They got him back."

He smiled. "Good, now the question is, can you leave them to do their work?"

She glared at him. "I wasn't interfering," she snapped. "You were asking all of your questions."

"We were, and we still have to," Gideon shared, "so that we can get to the bottom of this."

She shook her head. "It's not fair that I got my brother

back after all this time, but we still don't have any answers. I can't have anything happen that'll hurt him and set him back even more."

Gideon looked through the window of the door and noted the medical team still inside the room. He shook his head. "Your brother would want to help us as much as possible."

She sucked in her breath at that and nodded slowly. "Have you talked to Mason or Tesla?" she asked. "They were talking about bringing Mason out of the coma today."

"I hope they do, but I haven't heard anything yet."

She nodded. "It would be lovely to think that this could be over soon, both finding Mason's shooter and the people who took Nicholas," she murmured. "However, every time I turn around, something else is happening. Yet something is going on that's just plain ugly."

Gideon confirmed, "An awful lot of ugly is in this world, but we don't have to let it affect us."

She snorted at that. "Sounds great, but, at the moment, it seems like a bunch of malarkey," she muttered. "And, if you're anything like the investigators I had to work with before Masters showed up"—she shook her head in weariness—"we won't get along at all."

"We'll get along just fine," Gideon stated, with a smile, "because we are united in some important aspects."

She turned and said, "Enlighten me."

"We want to know what happened to your brother, and we don't want those assholes coming back for another round, with anyone."

Her eyes widened, as if she hadn't realized that could be a distinct possibility. She firmed up her lips and gave him a clipped nod. "That is very true. So I guess it's your job to go find these bastards," she muttered.

"Which is why I'm asking you if he told you anything helpful."

"No, but I wish he had. All he told me was that he was on his way home one day, and he was grabbed, beaten, and thrown into the back of a vehicle. I think then he was hit over the head or something." She frowned. "Afterward he was a captive and at their mercy during those four months. My God, who the hell keeps anybody for four months?"

"Only people who are either desperate or have a big potential payout," Gideon replied. "That's why we have to sort this out because we need to know about anybody who got those big bucks. We want to know what that payout is for and to ensure they never get it because, to do this once, just means they'll do it again and again. Anytime something works for someone, you can bet they'll quickly put it on repeat. Plus, it won't be long before the copycats start showing up."

She stared at him, uncomprehending for a moment, then noting how he considered this a real possibility. "That's disgusting."

"It's also human nature," he stated. "You and I both know that."

Jasper joined them now, and, by the looks of it, he already knew what had happened here. He came right to Elizabeth. Gideon gave Jasper a nod of acknowledgment, and Jasper smiled at him and then beamed at her.

"You trust him?" she demanded of Jasper, yet glancing at Gideon.

Jasper smiled and nodded. "Yes, I sure do." He eyed her carefully. "I've worked with Gideon many times. He's a good man."

She looked back over at him, but the distrust in her eyes never eased. "Maybe so, but I'll believe it when I get answers here."

"You got the best answer possible," Jasper noted, as he reached out and held her hand. "Remember when we first met, and your brother wasn't on anybody's radar but yours, and this guy," he said, as he pointed to Gideon, "was on a case somewhere out of the country."

She winced at that. "Thanks for the reminder," she muttered, "though I don't even want to go back to that part. My brother was worth absolutely everything, yet nobody, not even his own damn team, gave a shit."

"Which is something that we're looking into as well," Jasper declared.

She stopped and asked curiously. "You're investigating your own team?"

He gave her a flat stare, then turned to Gideon.

Gideon nodded. "If that's what occurred, then that's what we'll do. If nobody had Nicholas's back for all those months, you can damn well better believe I'll find out why," he stated, as Jasper nodded in agreement. "That'll never go down well for any of us."

She nodded. "Nicholas would never have thought such a thing could even happen. His whole career, he always firmly believed his people would have his back, but honestly, they've let him down in a big way, as far as I'm concerned," she said sadly. "It will be hard for him when he comes out of this and realizes just how badly they let him down and the price he paid for that."

"So, don't tell him right away," Gideon suggested. "He'll need to keep his spirits up on his long road to recovery. It won't be easy, and he will spend many months getting out of this, but he is clearly strong and capable. He survived some of the worst things that anybody could ever have survived. So let's give him the best chance on making a full recovery, while not pouring all this negativity back into his world."

She hesitated. "He'll ask."

"If he asks, then we'll tell him. We'll be honest," Jasper interjected. "We will say anything that needs to be said, without making it too difficult for him. Yet he doesn't need to know everything right now. Let's keep the man alive first, before we kill him with the additional news."

She winced at his phraseology and nodded. "To be honest, that's always worried me, thinking it would be one of the worst betrayals ever. So, find out why the hell all his supposed friends walked away from him," she murmured. "Maybe then he'll at least understand it."

"Will do," Gideon vowed, with half a smile. He smacked Jasper's arm, "Time to go."

Jasper nodded. "You're right." He gave her a smile. "We'll be back."

"You won't wait around and see if he'll be okay?"

Gideon smiled. "I already know he'll be okay. You just stay here and be there for him when he wakes up again." And, with that, Gideon turned to walk out, knowing that Jasper would follow.

Down the hallway, as they headed for the stairs, Jasper asked, "How do you know that he'll be okay?"

"Because he's a fighter, and I watched them as they brought him back. It didn't take a whole lot. For whatever reason, his blood pressure was all over the place. It's probably coming from his gut, some internal bleeding they didn't quite fix or something." Gideon shook his head. The human body could be such a fragile thing, and that amazed him the most. "But they will fix it, they'll get on it, and he will be fine. I refuse to tolerate anything less."

Jasper burst into laughter and grinned at him. "Sometimes we just need a hard-ass attitude, … even when directed at our own health."

"Yeah, and sometimes that hard-ass attitude doesn't do a damn bit of good."

"Maybe, but then you have to wonder if it isn't all about attitude, making sure that yours is the one that works in this world," Jasper offered. "You can think all kinds of things, but, at the end of the day, most of what happens in your life is what you believe, and *that* is something we can control."

"So, we do our best with whatever we are given, *huh*?"

"Exactly."

CHAPTER 3

THE REST OF the afternoon Pearl buried herself in work, forgetting the headache of the busybody out in the front office and the reappearance of Gideon. The only problem was that Gideon was much harder to put out of her mind. The fact that he was even here both terrified and delighted her because it was one thing to hold on to a wish, hoping to make something happen someday, and another thing entirely to have the opportunity. This situation was one where she would have to step out of that comfortable shell she had built up around herself and make it happen.

The *making it happen* part was a whole lot harder, and something she wasn't sure she was capable of, which just pissed her off because that's why she was here in town. Yet, when push came to shove, she wasn't sure she would have the guts to talk to him. Did she have what it took to say, *Hey, Gideon, should we try again?* Did she want to try again, or was that all just part and parcel of the same dreams she'd sucked herself into believing? Was it possible that it could happen again for the two of them? She felt like a fool when she considered it, and it became one more thing to bury in the distant recesses of her mind. She would have to deal with it, but right now was not the time.

When she finally finished work and headed out to the parking lot, she got into her vehicle and slowly drove home. Everything seemed normal, except, to her, it was all in technicolor, so amplified and so unexpected. She wasn't at all sure she was ready to deal with Gideon. As she pulled into her neighborhood, she looked around to see if she knew anyone, but it was calm and quiet, the street bare. The roadway was completely empty, which she expected.

She never thought she would face traumatic stress over seeing Gideon again, yet here she was, figuring out how to get out of creating the very life she had always wanted for herself—a life with him. The fact that she wanted it now, and they were both right here in the same city, all made her worry once again that maybe it was just a dream state that just sounded great but wasn't something she wanted bad enough to try for.

As she walked up to her front door, she stopped and looked around, feeling something off. She took a slow turn around, only to see what appeared to be nothing. Frowning, she took another step toward her door. Not liking anything about it, she turned and walked away. She got right back into her vehicle and drove away. Suddenly feeling ridiculous, she drove around the block, then pulled over to the curb a bit down the street, still trembling as she stared up at her house.

What the hell was going on?

Why the hell was somebody—and maybe not somebody, maybe it was all in her head—but it seemed as if something was wrong. She sat here, gasping for breath, calming down the chaos inside her, but it wasn't working. She couldn't force herself to go into her house or even to get out of her car again.

What the hell was going on, and what was wrong with her?

As she sat here a few more minutes, she watched another vehicle drive slowly up toward her place. She watched in amazement as her coworker, Betty, the woman who obviously had it in for her, drove right to her curb, got out, and walked quickly up to her front door. Instead of ringing the doorbell, she dropped something on the front step and then ran back to her car and raced away.

But who the hell had been here earlier, their lingering presence giving Pearl the impression that it wasn't safe to go into her own house? She frowned as she waited. Just when she was about to force herself to get out and to walk to her door, the front door opened just a crack, and she stared at the stranger in her home, as he snagged up whatever Betty had left on the porch and dragged it inside.

Shocked, Pearl wondered what some man was doing in her house to begin with. Then she spotted a strange man walking the neighborhood, dressed in civilian clothes. Granted, she didn't know her neighbors, but now she was getting paranoid. Too scared to deal with whatever was happening, yet not sure who to contact, her fingers automatically dialed the number that she knew from a long time ago. When Gideon answered, she closed her eyes, feeling the tears, the relief, and the pain clogging her voice. "Oh, thank God," she choked out.

"Pearl?" he asked in a hard tone. "Is that you? Pearl, talk to me," he snapped.

"Yes, yes, it's me," she replied, after an uncomfortable silence.

"At least you're talking," he muttered. "What's going on? Why did you call?" She didn't know what to say or even how to begin. "Pearl," he repeated, his tone suddenly all business and allowing no argument.

"Somebody is in my house right now," she whispered, "and I don't know why or how."

After a brief silence, he barked, "Start at the beginning."

"I'm parked nearby outside my place," she whispered, her voice trembling, "because I couldn't enter my house. It felt wrong, like so wrong. So I drove away, then felt stupid, so I pulled back around. Now I was sitting here in my car, just figuring out why I can't go into my own home, when one of the women I work with drove up to my house and walked up to my front door. Now, for a little backstory, you've got to understand that this woman hates my guts for some reason, and I don't know why. She dropped something on the front step, then left real fast. While I watched, not even a full minute later, my door opened, and a guy grabbed whatever Betty left there and snatched it back into the house. Plus, I saw some strange man walking the neighborhood, yet I didn't see a parked car anywhere. Maybe I'm just being paranoid."

"Did you know either of the two guys?"

"No."

"Who else lives there with you?"

She muttered, "I live alone."

"What's the address?" he asked briskly, wasting no time. "And where are you right now?"

"I'm still sitting in my car, a couple houses away and across the street. I just don't know what to do."

"You stay there. Don't get out," he ordered, and she heard his rushing footsteps. "I'll be there in a minute."

When her phone went dead, she stared at it, realizing she had probably called the one person in the world she could count on unconditionally, but jeez. Of all the people to call, he would be the most difficult to deal with. Yet she couldn't help smile because he was coming. It seemed as if no time had passed between them, and he was here to help her, even though some very unpleasant conversations were up ahead. Yet she ultimately wanted this, so, in a way, whatever was going on at her house was advancing her own personal plans. Still, never in her wildest dreams would she have planned something so bizarre as this.

When a vehicle pulled up a few minutes later, she watched as Gideon stepped out of the car, and, with an unhurried look, strolled up the block and got into the passenger seat of her car, sitting beside her. "You still don't lock the damn doors, do you?"

She blinked, realizing that she hadn't. She shrugged. "I could have said that I left it unlocked for you, which you wouldn't like either, would you?"

"No, because it would be a lie." He glanced at her and then stared ahead, as he spoke in a formal tone. "You're looking well."

"Not right now I'm not." The tears gathering at the back of her throat choked her voice. "I don't know what's going on."

"No, and we have a lot of that happening right now," he stated, with a nod. "So, did you recognize the person in the house?"

"No, not at all. I didn't get a great look at him, but still enough to know I don't know him. I can't even imagine."

"Don't even imagine right now," he said, with a quirk of his lips. "Let's just deal with one issue at a time."

"I would love to," she murmured, "but I don't know what's going on."

"Did you tell anybody that I was here?"

She shook her head. "No, no way. I'm still adjusting to the fact that you are here."

"Yeah, I was a bit surprised too. The guy I was with—"

She cut him off mid-sentence. "I don't know anything about what else may be going on."

"Did you talk to anybody at work today?"

"Yes, while I did my job." She frowned, thinking hard and fast, but coming up empty. "Other than that, I don't know what you mean by *talk to anybody*."

"Did you see anything unusual happen at work today?"

She blinked at that, thought about it, then shrugged. "No. I work in physiotherapy, so I'm not in the regular population of the hospital. Obviously I saw you in the stairwell, and that was a freaky scenario, particularly considering I'm the one who left last time," she shared, with a half laugh, unsure of what more to say about the sorry situation.

"You sure did," he confirmed in a causal tone, "and, as it was, we both ended up leaving."

"Yet here we both are again," she noted, with a questioning look.

"I came here to help a friend with a case, but this isn't where I've been living, not for a long time. I just flew in today."

She didn't say anything, just nodded.

"So, back to what's going on here," Gideon began. "Did you talk to anybody, see anything odd, different, unique in any of the places that you went to today?"

"None that I can think of," she said cautiously. "If you gave me something a little more specific, I might remember something. I'd had a tough day with a coworker spreading lies about me, which was fairly upsetting, so I stuck to myself."

"Why would they spread lies about you?"

"I don't know." She raised her hands in exasperation. "She's got it in for me, and nobody seems to want to stand up to her. She's one hell of a troublemaker, spreads all kinds of lies, and, if I were to guess, she could get away with murder and, well, I'm just stuck in the middle."

He shook his head. "That's not like you."

"No, it isn't. It's not like me to stick around when shit like that happens," she agreed, with a bitter tone. "I would much prefer to have a decent work environment, and I don't have that right now." He pondered it for a few minutes and when he didn't say anything, she asked, "What's that look for? Do you think I deserve it or something?"

Surprised, he shook his head. "Hell no. Why would you even say that? You've always been one of the most professional people I've ever met. I can't imagine how you would end up with somebody who hated you so much. That's all I was thinking."

Pearl added, "This woman's got it in for me."

"Any chance that she would do something to hurt you?"

Her stomach twisted. "I wouldn't have thought so, but I don't know what she was doing here or what she just delivered to my house. It didn't look as if she was necessarily delivering it in a nice way."

"What do you mean?"

"It was fast, as if she were skulking around. She raced up to the front door, dropped the package on the front stoop, and then left in a hurry."

"You don't think it was meant for the person inside?"

"That's seems far-fetched, but I don't know. To have two weird things happening at once is crazy too," she murmured. "Honestly, I don't know what the hell to even think at this point."

"It's all right. We'll get to the bottom of it."

"I hope so," she muttered, unsure of the conversation now. "Look. I don't know what you'll do here or in what way this could have anything to do with you and why you came to town, but I do appreciate the fact that you came to help me."

He nodded. "I appreciate the fact that you called. That couldn't have been easy."

"No, it wasn't," she admitted. "Still, foolish of me for making it difficult." She shrugged. "It seems as if a lot of things have been difficult these last few years."

"I'm sorry," he said. "That's not what I would have wished for you."

She shrugged and stared at her front door. "So, what the hell is going on in my house?"

"Do you own it?"

"No, I don't. I rent," she replied absentmindedly. "I've been here now for quite a few months though, so it's not as if I have an absentee owner or somebody coming back—not without some notice given to me."

"I wonder if it's a case of mistaken identity."

She asked hopefully, "That would be good though, wouldn't it?"

He shrugged. "Maybe, though they still moved into your house. Somebody is skulking around delivering something. Plus, he opened the door immediately and brought it in. That's all strange. Would your security camera have picked it up?"

"Yes," she said, but then shook her head. "I don't even know why I didn't think of that," she muttered, as she brought up her security system on her phone. She tapped the screen so it would play, then she handed him the phone. "There. That's my coworker Betty."

"The one who hates you?"

"Yes, the one who hates me."

They watched as she raced up to the front door, looking around in that furtive manner, then dropped whatever it was on the front step, before taking off again.

Gideon nodded. "Definitely furtive, definitely not sure she should be there, and yet, in one way or another, heavily involved in whatever this is."

They waited and watched the security video as the person inside her house opened the door and grabbed whatever had been left.

"That also is very bizarre."

"It makes no sense." She turned to stare back at the house. "None of it makes any sense."

"It will," he murmured. "It always does at the end of the day."

She turned to him and nodded. "I guess that's why I called you. This is the stuff you do, isn't it?"

"Oh, it's definitely some of the stuff I do," he murmured. "Though I can't say this is exactly the stuff I do because this is weird and bizarre, even for me."

"Ya think?" she quipped, with a headshake. "I just don't understand. Nothing here makes any sense."

"It will," he stated calmly. "It will. It's just that we'll need a few minutes to figure it out." He pulled out his phone and contacted somebody on the other end.

"Look. I'm here at Pearl's house." And he recited her address. "She's got a strange male in her house whom she doesn't recognize. Somebody came by, delivered a parcel.

Pearl knows the person who delivered the parcel, but the woman delivering it is furtive and sneaky, and they've had workplace issues," he explained, "so we're not sure what kind of scenario we have here, but definitely a stranger is in her house."

She listened to the one-sided conversation with great interest, as Gideon went on.

"Can you check to see if anybody has reported anything suspicious in the neighborhood?" He turned to her, then smiled, noting Pearl's worried expression. "It's okay. It's just Jasper, the guy I work with."

She nodded and slumped in her seat, as she returned her attention to her house. "It makes no sense," she muttered.

"Remember that it will later. We just don't know enough yet."

She nodded and didn't say anything, as the two men talked.

"Okay, I'll go in and see if we can flush him out." She stared at him in alarm, but he just smiled reassuringly, as he finished his call. "Okay," he told Pearl. "I'll go have a look around. I want you to stay here, and I don't want you to open this door. Keep both doors locked," he stated pointedly, "and I'll be back in a few minutes."

"But what if he sees you?"

He smiled. "It will be a good thing if he sees me, won't it?"

She frowned. "I don't know what he's doing here, Gideon. What if he's got a gun?"

"Then he damn well better use it," Gideon replied, "because I don't take kindly to strangers hiding away in women's houses. Just give me a minute." He gave her a brief smile and added hurriedly, "Nice to see you, by the way."

With that, he slipped out of the car and slipped up to her house.

NOBODY'D BEEN MORE surprised when Pearl had called than Gideon, but, as soon as he realized what the issue was, he'd come running. He knew he always would, and something about this damsel-in-distress situation was totally his thing. They always got to him, especially this damsel. However, he was desperate to keep Pearl alive and well. Seeing how she had been years before and seeing her now was like time had just completely skipped over her.

She was still beautiful in that same breathtaking way. Listening to the story she had to tell, initially he wondered if she were delusional. Now, having seen the video, he knew something was going on here that made absolutely no sense.

Of course he couldn't get the idea out of his head that it might be connected to Mason's shooting, the nightmare in his world that he had been called to help out with, Yet he knew of no real reason for these two events to be connected. Still, how many times did things like this happen with people in the same area? He walked away from her house to circle around the block, judging when he was close to being on the back side of her house. He slipped into the neighbor's backyard and headed for Pearl's backyard.

He quickly jumped over the neighbor's wire fence, which led to an empty backyard. Satisfied with that, he walked alongside the wooden fence of Pearl's backyard, as close as he could get, then quickly jumped over the wooden fence and approached Pearl's house from the back. Walking up to one of the windows, he pressed his ear against the wall to see if he could hear anything. A conversation was going on, but, from the sound of it, it was one-sided, likely a phone call.

"No, she's not home yet. ... I don't know why we had to pick her place anyway. You should see what the hell somebody delivered to her front door. This girl has already got enemies. ... It's like one of the most malicious cards you've ever seen, definitely high school BS," he explained. "I'm thinking that we don't want to get involved with this. ... No, we're not involved, but yeah, yeah, yeah, whatever." He groaned. "I'm right here, waiting for whenever you're ready to get your shit down here, so we can get this done." He ended the call, then muttered, "Bloody unbelievable."

Gideon figured that comment was related to whatever was in the delivery parcel.

"Christ, that woman has got to be nuts."

Gideon wasn't sure which woman the intruder was referring to. Now hearing footsteps, Gideon took a chance and peered in the window, only to see the stranger walking from the kitchen into the other room. So Gideon moved toward the back door, and, finding it unlocked, he slipped inside.

He moved quickly to where the intruder had been standing and checked out the area, looking to see where he'd gone. He found him in the living room, staring out the front window, waiting impatiently for whatever was to come. Gideon just didn't know what that was.

The man turned suddenly and caught sight of Gideon standing there. The stranger stared at him, then roared, "Who the hell are you, and what are you doing here?"

"More to the point," Gideon replied, stepping closer, "I'm supposed to be here. Now, who the hell are you, and what are you doing here? You're trespassing."

"So are you," he declared, with venom in his tone. "That bitch lives alone."

"Is that who you're waiting for?" he asked in a soft tone.

The other guy shrugged. "No, I don't give a shit about her. What does it matter to me? She's supposed to be some uptight broad, so I don't give a fuck."

"So why are you here, and what the hell are you doing messing up her world?" As Gideon took another step forward, the intruder pulled out a handgun.

Gideon looked at it and nodded. "I wondered why you were hiding out in a woman's house, without a weapon, unless you thought you could just overpower her," he stated calmly, as he stared at the guy. "I can't say I appreciate any asshole who'll do that."

"Hey, it's not about overpowering her. I'm here for something else."

"Yeah? I don't believe you, and you're here trespassing in a woman's house, with a gun now." He pointed at the intruder's weapon. "As far as I'm concerned, I'm thinking the worst, and so will the cops."

"Except the cops won't find me," he declared, as he lifted the gun.

"Ah, so you think you will skip, *huh*? You think that shooting me won't bring all kinds of trouble on your head?"

"If it does, I won't be here to face it," he declared.

Something about the guy's tone made Gideon realize that he believed it. That meant one of two things. Either the intruder had someone else coming fast or he had an out from this that would get him away or off the hook. "I'm not sure who's been getting you off the hook so far," Gideon admitted, "but that's about to come to an end."

The other guy laughed and laughed. "As if you even

know what you're talking about." He smirked. "All kinds of things in this world you don't understand, and you've just stuck your nose into something that you shouldn't have."

"If you hadn't got caught sneaking into a woman's house," he noted, with a smile that exuded confidence, "you wouldn't have failed. But now you're the failure, and there'll be a penalty for that."

The other guy shook his head. "You're just trying to stress me out."

"Sure, I am. I'm wondering whether this is connected to something else or you're just one of those slimeballs who likes to rape women."

The other guy paled, then burst out in a fury, "I don't have to rape nobody. I needed this bitch's house, that's all."

At that, Gideon didn't know what to say. He considered some angles, then asked curiously, "So it didn't matter who lived here?"

"No, I don't give a fuck who lives here," he snapped. "All I needed was her property."

"What about the parcel you picked up out front?"

At that, the guy started to laugh. "Oh my God, I don't know what the hell's going on with that. I saw the woman who delivered it, and I didn't want to just leave it out there to attract attention, so I brought it inside, but wow." The gunman shook his head. He took a moment and laughed again, the gun still pointed at Gideon. "That is one seriously twisted mind."

"What did she leave?" he asked curiously.

"Some nasty, insulting shit. Whoever that woman is, she's got a serious problem."

"She's not working with you?"

He shook his head. "No, she isn't, though I should say

yes, so she would get picked up and interrogated," he shared, again laughing. "Regardless you won't live long enough to tell anybody." With that, he casually shifted his gun hand, but Gideon was already on the move.

CHAPTER 4

P EARL SAT OUTSIDE for the longest moments, just
waiting, her heart in her throat as she wondered what
the hell was going on inside. When her phone rang, she
frowned to see a number she didn't know. Hesitantly she
answered it.

"My name is Jasper. I'm a friend of Gideon's."

"Yes, yes, he mentioned your name when he got off the
phone earlier."

"That's correct. What's going on there?"

"I haven't heard from him since he went to check out
the house." She anxiously clutched the phone in her hand.
"I'm just sitting here, waiting, but I don't know what's going
on."

"You just keep waiting," Jasper said. "I want you to stay
right where you are. A group of men will soon enter your
house, so I don't want you to move. We can't have you
becoming part of this."

"I'm not part of it," she said in frustration, "but Gideon
went in there at least ten or fifteen minutes ago, and he
hasn't come out."

"I've been in contact with him, and I just need you to
stay where you are."

She took several slow, deep breaths. "Fine, but somebody sure as hell better get me some answers before I go in there on my own."

"Do *not* go in there," Jasper snapped.

She glared down at the phone. "Fine, but the longer you take, the harder it is for me to sit here. I'm worried about Gideon."

"I don't care how hard it is for you to sit there," Jasper replied, his tone inflexible. "Do not move from that car, do you hear me? I don't have the manpower to waste on sending somebody over there to sit in that car with you. Make sure you stay put. I can't afford to take people away from what's going on inside that house."

"That's fine," she muttered, sagging back into her seat. "Just make sure that Gideon's okay."

First came silence on the other end. "That, I can do," he said calmly, then quickly ended the call.

She stared down at her phone, wondering what Gideon could possibly have told Jasper that he would even think to call her. Yet it made sense that he would, as she remembered how Gideon had used her name in the earlier call to Jasper. So he was in contact with Gideon, so surely he was okay. He had to be okay.

Anything else just wasn't acceptable. She sat here with her face buried in her hands. When a knock came at her driver's side window, she shrieked and looked up to see Gideon. She immediately unlocked her door and bolted out of the car, throwing herself into his arms. "Oh my God, oh my God," she cried out. "Are you okay?"

He held her close and murmured, "I'm fine. I'm okay."

She patted his body to confirm he wasn't hurt and then asked, "What the hell happened? You went in there and then nothing."

"Definitely not nothing," he replied, with a grimace, "but not anything you want to hear."

"Oh, no, I want to hear it. I need to know what the hell is going on."

"Come in the house then."

She nodded and locked up her car, then turned to Gideon. "What about the guy inside? Did you get him?" He winced at that. She stopped in her tracks, shocked. "Did you kill him?" she asked.

"It's not so much that *I* killed him but that his own actions led to his death."

She frowned, as he led her slowly up to the house. "What the hell does that mean?"

"It means," a man replied from her front step, which startled her. But the man gave her a smile, a friendly face. "It means that the intruder fired his gun, thinking Gideon would be an easy target, and found out the opposite."

She looked over at Gideon in panic. "But you weren't hurt?"

"I'm not hurt," he repeated.

"But he shot you," she cried out in confusion.

"No, he shot *at* me. I don't kill very easily, remember?"

She blinked at that, remembering bits and pieces of stories she had heard. "Oh my God."

He wrapped his arm around her shoulders and tucked her up close. "It's fine."

"No, it's not fine," she argued, taking several deep breaths, "but it will be."

"Exactly." He gave her a quick squeeze. "Now come on. I need you to see something."

"I'm coming, but I can't say I'll be too impressed if my

house is destroyed."

"What do you call *destroyed*?" he asked curiously.

She glared at him as he opened her front door, and she winced at the massive blood puddle just inside her house, and yet no body was here. "Where is he?" she asked, looking around. "I want to see his face."

"That's why I want you to see if you recognize him."

She was led out to the backyard, where she saw a whole team of people working. Sure enough, an ambulance had arrived silently, and a gurney sat inside it, with the body completely zipped up atop it. All of a sudden, it was way too real. She sucked back her breath, sagging against Gideon. She was freaked out, just now realizing that she never heard any sirens. She had been so self-absorbed in all this that she never even realized when all these people arrived, even though she had been sitting right outside.

"It's all right," Gideon said. "This guy was waiting inside the house *for you*."

She blinked at that and slowly nodded. "I do have to remember that, don't I?" She was in limbo, wanting him dead and *not* wanting him dead. "Otherwise I'll feel so damn bad."

"You can't feel bad in this case," Gideon murmured. "This guy was in your house, waiting for you, but we still don't know why."

"And neither do I," she replied in bewilderment. "It makes no sense to me."

"Well, first let's see if you recognize him." As they walked to the gurney, Gideon kept his arms locked around her for support. When they got up to the body, he asked, "Are you ready?"

She just nodded. The EMT unzipped the black bag, and

she stared down at the face of the man who'd been here in her home. Bewildered, she shook her head. "I don't know him at all. I don't understand. Why was he in my house?"

"We'll talk about that inside," Gideon said, as he turned and led her back into the kitchen.

She sagged down onto a kitchen chair and stared up at him.

"As much as nobody wants to consider it, I did find out that he wasn't here to rape you," he shared, and she stared at him in shock.

"That's the good news, I guess," she replied cautiously. "If that's not the reason, why was he there?"

"He told me that he *needed the house.*"

Dumbfounded, she couldn't even begin to make sense of what he was talking about.

Gideon nodded. "That sounds strange to me too, so we're wondering if anything is going on with your neighbors here."

"With my neighbors?" she asked, staring at him. She got up and walked to the living room window, where she stared outside her house. "I don't even know my neighbors. I've only been here at this particular house, ... I don't know, maybe eight months." Then she frowned. "I guess in most places you could get to know people in that time, but I'm always at work. Plus, if I'm not at work, I'm at the gym, or I'm at home. I guess I haven't been terribly friendly because I don't know anybody here."

"Okay, that's important, and again, you don't recognize him? Not at all?"

"No, not at all."

"Now think about it before you answer my next question. What about this?" He pointed to the little gift bag that was on her kitchen table.

She stared at it and winced. "That's from Betty, isn't it?"

He nodded. "Yes, as far as we can tell, and I did ask your intruder about it," he shared, with a forced calm tone, but she knew his triggers. "He told me that she had nothing to do with anything he was up to, which is too bad, because I would love for her to be found guilty of something." Pearl stared at him, and he shook his head at the irony. "You need to take a look at it."

Frowning, she opened it up and inside was a card and a small bottle of something that looked rather putrid. "What is it?" she asked, frowning, then smelled the top of the bottle. Even closed, it had an acrid smell.

Gideon shook his head. "I don't know, but I suspect, if you would open that up, it won't smell the nicest."

She looked at the card and read out loud. "*You're such a bitch*, and there's a winking emoji. *I figured this is exactly what you deserve. Isn't it time you left your job and moved on?* Jeez, are we in junior high?" She stared at it, and then shook her head. "I have never met anybody like Betty in my life," she stated. "Mean and vindictive. Why would anyone go out of their way to do something like this?" The last part was a rhetorical question, but it was obviously on everyone's mind.

"She appears to be obsessed with you. The question is, why?" Gideon asked.

"I have no idea." Pearl raised both hands. "I don't even talk to her."

"We have video proof that she delivered this, so the question is, what is in the bottle, and do you even want to know?"

"No, I don't want to know," she declared. Still, she got a little bit closer to the bottle and wrinkled up her nose.

"Honestly, it smells like urine and poop."

Jasper joined them, and both the men shared a look. "That was our take."

"Why on earth?" she muttered.

"I don't know, but you appear to have somebody at your office with a serious mental problem."

"Ya think?" Pearl stared at it, turning all kinds of red with the fury overtaking her. "I don't need crap like this."

"None of us do," Gideon agreed, "but this is something that we can't leave unanswered either."

"Oh, *great*," she muttered, almost too loud for even herself, but she needed to vent, "because that'll bring me even more trouble."

"How will that get you in trouble?" Gideon asked.

"I don't know, but every time any complaint is made against her, she's been let off the hook."

The men eyed each other. Jasper asked, "Has she got any relationships with anybody at work?"

"I honestly don't know," she replied.

"More to the point, do *you* have any relationships at work?" Jasper asked carefully.

She frowned and shook her head. "No, I haven't gone out with anybody at work. I'm not a fan of workplace romances," she said, looking sideways at Gideon. "They get very, ... oh, let's go with *awkward*."

"Did you rebuff anybody at work?" Gideon asked.

She sagged back into her chair.

"You did, didn't you?"

"I mean, ... not badly. He wanted to go out for lunch, so I did, thinking it was just a quick coworker thing. Then he wanted to go out for dinner, and I told him that wasn't something I was interested in. I wasn't, and I'm still not. He seemed to take it fine, and I told him that I just didn't get involved with office romances to begin with, that it wasn't my thing, and that I liked him, but I didn't like him in that way."

"Did you make it very clear that your answer was no?" Jasper asked.

She nodded. "I thought so. It's hard not to have it be clear when you actually say the word *no*."

"Yet we all know that some people are deliberately obtuse," Jasper stated.

"Maybe, but that wouldn't have anything to do with this." She waved at the bottle of whatever it was and the nasty card. "Did she think that I wouldn't know who it was from?" She looked at the two men, puzzled.

"If she didn't know that you had a security system, then yes. It would make sense that she wouldn't expect to get caught."

She nodded blankly. "I've never in my life seen anybody do something like this."

"She's apparently a little unhinged when it comes to you."

"Ya think?" She hated that she seemed to be saying the same thing repeatedly, but it was all a little hard to process.

"Unless somebody else is putting her up to it."

She blinked at that too. "You mean, to get me fired or to get me to quit?"

"Then maybe you would go out with this guy you rebuffed."

She stared at him and laughed. "I wouldn't go out with him because I told him I didn't like him in that way. That's not the way this works."

"Maybe he didn't believe you, or maybe he just thought

that if he could get you away from the office and get you away from things that bothered you, he could convince you otherwise. You made it clear that you have a problem with work romances, after all."

She shook her head. "Seriously, nobody in my world gives a shit about me like that, and it makes no sense."

"At least we have some proof now."

"Yeah, that is good. Now Betty's been clearly caught on camera. So, now what? Do I call the police?" she asked, as she looked at the bottle, looked at the others. "Surely this can't go unanswered too."

"No," Gideon declared, looking over at Jasper, who nodded too. "This definitely doesn't go unanswered, but you also must realize that, if Betty loses her job, she's likely to take more steps in an unhinged direction."

Pearl buried her face in her hands, as she tried to figure out what the hell had just happened in her world. "I've been wondering if it was time to just pull up stakes and move." She seemed frazzled, and the fury was dampening with the reality crashing down on her.

"You're making that decision pretty easily," Jasper intervened.

"I would imagine that decision wouldn't be very hard at this point," Gideon countered. "Personally, I'm quite surprised to find you back here."

She just nodded, didn't say anything. How could she explain that she was back because of him? It made her sound almost as bad as whoever the hell was stalking her now. "Do we think that she's …" Pearl shook her head. She stared at the evidence before her, then panicked and looked back to the guys for support. "I just don't understand it."

"How bad has it been at work?"

"It's been bad for a while, but especially the past few weeks to a month, and then today? Well, today might have started this," she muttered, as she stared at the bottle, which looked like a urine sample from the labs, yet darker than it should be.

"Tell us about today."

"It wasn't any different than any other day," she began, "but then it got a little worse in some ways because I found out she was badmouthing me to everybody in the office. Even to the extent that at times the patients could hear her. I wasn't happy on a professional level to have her doing that in a work environment, but she's been told off about it before. Still, it's never seemed to make a difference. She got reprimanded today by the head of the therapy group."

"So, that's the extent of it?"

"She's never lost her job. I don't think she's even come close to having anybody even put her on probation," she muttered.

"So, somehow her job is protected," Jasper noted.

"That *somehow* is something we must figure out," Gideon stated, "because, as of now, you're not safe from her at work or at home. For all we know, that bottle's got something in it."

She stared at it, feeling her stomach recoil, and she nodded. "I think you're right," she agreed. "It would have to be tested to find out for sure. What probably set her off is the fact that my supervisor went to bat for me today with a reprimand because Betty was being particularly nasty and vile."

"Yeah, I can see how that would have set her off."

"*Great*, so I just can't win in this instance, can I?"

"The fact that she was here when we also had somebody

in your house is just aggravating our issue under investigation. Now we've got to confirm that she isn't connected to Mason's case somehow."

Pearl stared blankly. "I can't imagine that Betty was connected with Mason's sniper attack, but it isn't for me to say," she stated. "That will be for you guys to figure out. ... I don't suppose I could have you guys make an issue out of this little delivery, *huh*?" she asked, looking carefully from Gideon to Jasper, "So that I'm more or less out of it?"

"It won't matter if you're out of it or not. You'll get blamed in Betty's mind no matter what," Gideon stated, being straight with her. "You only have to look at how she's acted up until now."

Pearl whispered, "Jeez, this is just too much."

"We'll have to figure out in what way her job is protected and see if they've got anything to do with this harassment by Betty or even with Mason's shooting."

She shrugged. "We can call my supervisor. She is one of the most professional people I know, honest too. She might have an idea but isn't telling me. I don't know."

"What's her name?" Jasper asked.

She gave him the name and phone number of her direct boss and added, "It's best if I'm left out of this as much as possible."

"You *were* left out of this," Gideon pointed out, with a laugh. "You remained in your car, and I was with you. We saw the video. Betty brought this on herself," he declared, his tone hard. "I'm more concerned about what comes next as a workplace consequence and then what's Betty's reaction to you."

"Me too," Pearl muttered. "but it has to stop."

"Oh, it will stop now," Gideon murmured. "We just

don't know what will start up afterward."

THE PARCEL WAS one thing, and the unhinged coworker Betty was another thing, and both were completely different compared to whatever the asshole Gideon had killed was up to. He didn't even want to go through the details as to how the shooting had happened, and it had certainly happened quickly. The gunman pulled his gun quickly, just quick enough to get himself killed.

Gideon had already gone over the details with Jasper. Now that there had been a shooting, a full investigation would ensue. He was up for that regardless, and it was okay by him. This asshole tried to shoot him, and, as far as Gideon was concerned, it was self-defense all the way. He wasn't sure how Pearl would handle it, but she was still rather shell-shocked. She was also dealing with more than just one issue here, and the coworker problem alone was very strange.

Jasper whispered, "Better call Pearl's supervisor."

Gideon nodded because he wanted the same thing. He got up, stepped out on the back deck, and called her supervisor. When the woman answered on the first ring, he quickly identified himself as one of the investigators on base. He didn't give her much more information than that and got straight to the point. "I'm looking for contact information for a woman who goes by the name of Betty."

After a moment of silence, Maria asked carefully. "Why, if I may ask?"

"Sure, I'm keeping Pearl out of this, as she's dealing with enough shocks right now. What I can tell you at this point is that Betty has crossed the line, and I need her contact information right now."

"Oh dear, oh dear." Maria gasped for breath.

"Contact information," he repeated.

"Yes, yes, of course." She quickly gave him Betty's full name, address, and phone number. "I hope it's not serious."

"It appears Betty is being protected by somebody at work," Gideon added, without any reservation because there was no point in beating around the bush. "Do you know who that is?" She hesitated, and he understood her reaction, but he needed to assert his authority to speed things up a bit. "I'll be coming to your office very soon for an in-person interview on this matter, so the sooner you give me the information I need, the better."

"Oh dear, but that's, that's kind of ..."

Gideon interrupted her wanderings with a more forceful tone. "Betty's harassment of Pearl is not something you would want broadcasted. I get it, but, when I say Betty's crossed the line, she's crossed the criminal line and will be picked up and brought in for questioning very soon."

"Did she hurt Pearl?" Maria cried out in astonishment. "I thought for sure Betty was harmless."

"She may have been until she delivered something today to Pearl's house and then snuck away. We're having the contents of the bottle analyzed as we speak."

"Oh my gosh, I never thought anything like that would happen."

"According to Pearl, something may have happened earlier today that could have triggered this."

Silence came on the other end, and then Maria replied in a more professional tone, "I had to reprimand Betty more harshly than usual and even went to my boss again. Betty's been just an absolute bitch, completely unprofessional, and her actions should *never* be allowed," Maria stated, clearly upset. "But, for some reason, nothing I say or do ever seems to change it."

"Who's your boss?" Gideon asked immediately.

She gave him the name, then added, "You could get this information from other people, right?" She was worried, and it showed. "I'm not giving away anything?"

"No, of course not," Gideon replied. "Don't worry. This will wind up very official."

She asked again, "Is Pearl okay?"

"Yeah, just shaken up."

"Pearl is a sweetheart and has been one of our best employees. She's a wonderful physiotherapist. I know that all this has been incredibly troubling for her, and she's mentioned to me that she may very well leave because of it, but I was hoping we could get it stopped before she made that choice."

"I'm not sure what her state of mind is at the moment," Gideon shared, "but we'll get her to a safe place, where she can have some time to destress. Under the circumstances, she may not be in to work for the next few days, though I don't have an official ruling on that yet."

"I do need a little more information about you," she said carefully, "so that I'm not in trouble for passing on this information."

He quickly gave her his name, rank, and his contact number. "If you have any issues, my boss for the purpose of the current case regarding Betty would be Jasper Maclintok."

"Okay, good, thank you. Please tell Pearl to call me, whenever she feels up to it."

"I'll tell her that," Gideon said, then quickly ended the

call. He went back inside to see Jasper talking to Pearl. Gideon shared a knowing look with Jasper, who pulled out his phone and stepped away a little. Gideon addressed Pearl, "I talked to Maria. She seems to be a good boss to have on your side, but she's pretty freaked out about it all too."

"I'll bet she is. It's not her fault or anything she has control of. Betty is just nasty."

Gideon nodded. "Her behavior is inexcusable to me, and she should have been sent down the road a long time ago."

Pearl winced. "That's true, and Maria's done her best to deal with it, but, when management won't support Maria, what is she left to do?"

"I get it, and there will end up being a much bigger investigation because of what Betty did. She crossed a line."

Pearl shivered and nodded, and then smelled coffee, realized Jasper had put some on.

The smell eased Gideon's stretched nerves. "Coffee will be good," he said, with a note of humor. "Good choice."

She looked over at him, a wry look on her face. "You're still a coffee addict?"

"Are *you* still a coffee addict?" he replied, with a smile.

"I am, yes, the one bad habit I haven't been able to kick."

"It's the one bad habit I don't give a crap about kicking," Gideon declared, grinning.

She burst out laughing. "Trust you to make me feel like all those years we've been apart just disappeared. ... I didn't say it before, and I should have," she shared honestly, "but it's sure good to see you." He smiled a genuine smile that tugged on her heartstrings, as she realized just how much she'd lost.

He nodded. "Ditto, right back at you. And, just for the

record, you're looking great. Did I mention that earlier?"

She flushed bright red and then laughed. "Yeah, you mentioned it while I was sitting outside, freaking out. You always were good with compliments."

"Hey, I'm not good with anything. That's just the truth. You've always looked good. You always did. Just something about you is such a natural presence." He took another look at her, and she flushed again. "Just that *home girl beauty* thing."

She flushed and laughed. "As I said, always good with the compliments."

He shrugged. "But never for any other reason than the truth," he murmured. "It's the truth."

"Thank you." She gave him a bashful nod.

He got up, poured coffee for them, and handed her a cup. "How are you feeling?"

"Rough, to be honest. This is not exactly how I thought my day would end when I got up this morning," she shared. "It was rough at work because of … Betty. I was prepared to come home and to write up my notice, figuring out what was next in my life. It was rough when I saw you there in the hallway," she added, shaking her head. "That hit me like a ton of bricks."

"Hit you how?"

She looked over at Jasper and realized he was still on the phone and not paying attention, and that was as much privacy as she would likely get any time soon. "Because I realized just how much …" She winced. Forcing herself to be as honest with him as he had been with her—even knowing it might completely change everything—she went on. "Knowing what I lost."

He stared at her, his eyebrows shooting up. "Lost?"

"Yes, lost." She nodded, the sorrow evident in her expression. "I'm the one who broke us up. I'm the one who walked away, and I'm still not exactly sure why, except that … I just don't think I was ready for the commitment it seemed we were heading toward. I wasn't ready and, well, … I ran. I was terrified," she admitted, the shame and sorrow filling her heart.

Gideon still listened to her, but he never spoke up.

"Then today, when all this hell broke loose, I was getting ready to run yet again, only to realize how much time I spend running, and I didn't want to run anymore," she murmured. She stared down at her hands on her lap, lifted her gaze to his. "So I'm staying here, for whatever may happen. *With us.*"

IN THE CRAZINESS of the last couple hours, Pearl's words just washed over Gideon, adding to the confusing combination of it all. He didn't even know what to say, but he understood that she was sitting here, waiting for him to say something. It was the *something* part that he didn't have figured out yet.

When he didn't respond right away, she winced. "I would ask you to say something, anything," she said too quickly, "because the silence is deadly painful, but honestly, the silence also says everything."

"No, it doesn't," he countered. "You've caught me off guard. I hadn't had any clue that you were anywhere near here at all. I wasn't expecting to see you, and now that you're here, … you've thrown me for a loop."

"Yeah, I got that part," she noted, with a mocking laugh.

He stared at her, hearing the derision in her tone. "You didn't use to be so self-critical."

She shrugged. "Life hasn't been all that easy."

"What happened after you left? We lost touch."

"No, we didn't lose touch." She raised her hands to stop with the niceties. "Call it what it was. I walked away—ran away more like it—and I did reach out, but by then you'd left for overseas."

He nodded slowly. "I'll admit that the breakup was rough. It was fast. I thought we were heading down a path to a future together, with something permanent. The next thing I know, nothing is permanent because we no longer had a path. You were gone."

She nodded. "And I've explained that, although it's not much of an explanation. And I can certainly understand if you don't get it. I'm not sure I get it, but something about how things went today with Betty and then Maria had me wanting to leave it all again to start fresh. Then I realized how much of my world was about running away."

"Was talking to me so hard that you had to run away?" he asked. "I thought we had a great relationship, with good communication, until you suddenly just left. I realized that maybe we didn't have anything at all." Gideon watched the wisp of regret cross her face. "I'm not trying to make you feel bad. I'm just ... I still don't understand."

"I'm not sure that understanding is even something I can give you," she murmured, "because honestly, it's not an explanation that comes easily. I wasn't ready for a commitment, and I didn't think I was ready for anything, and now here I am, ... in another mess of my own making, though I'm not entirely sure what I did to deserve it."

"It doesn't mean that you did anything to deserve it," he

declared. "You didn't use to blame yourself for everything."

"No, I didn't," she agreed, with a smile, "and then, over time, you start to look at all the things you've done wrong and realize that you're the reason you're alone and not liking your life very much. I was living with more regrets than joy and happy memories. ... Anyway"—she seemed to give herself a physical shake and looked back at him—"I'm happy to let it go. I just needed to tell you."

"And I appreciate that." Gideon placed his hand on his heart. "I'm not exactly sure what to do with that information, and you sprang it on me, but I do appreciate that you spoke up. It's always good to know what happened."

She nodded. "I suppose I will have an interview with your boss now."

Gideon knew her head was just not in the game. "Yes. We must deal with the problem of Betty."

Pearl frowned at that and then shrugged. "That seems so minor when compared to everything else."

"And maybe it is minor, but we can't take a chance. If it's all connected somehow to Mason's shooting event—and that's a big *if*—we must follow up."

"You think that Betty brought that package for my intruder to collect? I don't think so. Yet, if she did, somehow the intruder could be involved in Mason's shooting? That doesn't make any sense either."

"Maybe not, but it's also possible that somebody else saw Betty come by."

"Meaning?"

"Your intruder may not be acting alone. If he or his partner were afraid that Betty saw something, when dropping off your package, maybe they would want to shut up Betty too."

Pearl stared at him, and her jaw slowly dropped, as she realized what he was saying. "You think Betty's life could be in danger?"

"It could be. We just don't know. Regardless, I do have to follow up, and I have to go see Maria's boss as well."

Pearl nodded, as she stared around at her house. "I can't stay here, can I?"

"No, you can't, but that will just be for a few hours at best or a few days at most," Gideon explained, with a careless wave. "Do you have a friend's place you can go to?"

She shook her head. "No, I don't." She huddled and wrapped her arms around her chest. "I can go to a hotel, I guess." She stared around aimlessly, still in shock, not quite sure what she was supposed to do.

Just then Jasper rejoined them. Looking from one to the other, he gauged the chill. "Are you two okay?"

Gideon nodded. "Phone calls made?"

"Yeah. The guys are on the Mason investigation, trying to find leads, witnesses. Meanwhile, I told them that you were tasked with the Pearl investigation, to see if it linked up to Mason somehow. Both investigations will share intel daily. We'll drop off Betty's delivery for analysis later today. I stepped aside to give you guys a few minutes, though I'm not sure you settled anything," he noted, his gaze going from one to the other.

"Not a whole lot to settle," she replied briefly. "I can't stay here, can I?"

"No, you can't," he confirmed immediately, and she just nodded.

Gideon looked over at Jasper. "I just told her that, but she was hoping for a different response."

"It can't be, not after your armed intruder was killed

here. This is now a crime scene," he declared, with a shake of his head. "Pack a bag, and we'll get you to a hotel, where you can stay tonight."

"Will one night be enough?" she asked, staring at him. "What about work? What do I do about that?"

Gideon nodded. "I already told your boss that chances are you won't be coming in for a couple days, but, yes, you do need to check in with her too."

When Pearl just stared at Gideon, he could see that none of this was filtering through. Groaning, he reached for her hand. "Come on. Let's get you upstairs, where we can pack a bag."

She immediately rose from her chair, yet just stood there, dumbstruck.

Gideon turned to Jasper, who was staring at her, frowning. "She'll be fine," Gideon said. "She's just had a difficult day."

"Ya think?" he asked, with a sideways look. "I'm not sure we should leave her alone like this. Does she have somebody to look after her?"

She immediately turned, her expression flat. "I'll be just fine." She waved her hand. "I've been alone a lot in my life, so don't worry about it."

That comment surprised Gideon, since Pearl had always been surrounded by friends and family when he knew her before. He wasn't sure when all these changes happened. She was never alone when they were together. "Look. If nothing else, you can come stay at my place. I have a spare room."

She stared at him for a long moment and then shook her head. "No, thanks. A hotel would be good."

For some reason her rejection hit him harder than it should have, considering the situation. It was certainly her right after all, particularly given their history, but it seemed to be more than that. He looked over at Jasper again, who was almost waiting for Gideon to respond, but he shook his head. "Come on. Let's get you packed."

He wasn't sure that he would let her go to a hotel, not when she was as obviously upset and out of it as she appeared to be right now. He would also get damn angry if she was refusing his offer of help just because of what she'd shared a few moments ago.

He would like to think that, if nothing else, they were still friends. He understood that she might feel awkward about it all, but he hadn't had any time to process things. So she could be as awkward as she wanted. It still wouldn't change the fact that it wasn't the way things would go down.

He marched her to her bedroom and waited while she collected a bag of clothing. She took enough for more than a few days, maybe a week or two. He was quite surprised, until he realized she was literally grabbing things and throwing them into the bag, with no apparent rhyme or reason as to what she was collecting. Finally he got up, grabbed another bag from the closet, then handed it to her and watched as she basically packed up all her clothing.

When she stood here with her two bags, she just looked at them blankly.

"Shoes," he nudged.

She nodded, then headed to the closet, where she pulled out a pair of runners and a couple pairs of walking shoes.

"Do you expect to go back to work anytime soon?" he asked her.

She thought about it, then shook her head. "I have no idea, and I'm not sure if I even want to."

"No, of course not," he stated. "I suspect that's taken on

a negative connotation for you."

She didn't say anything but looked around with that same blank expression.

He nudged her to the bathroom. "Grab a few toiletries."

Within seconds, everything was packed up, almost a clean sweep. Probably a few things were around that she would still want, but she had essentially packed up all her personal stuff from her bedroom and wouldn't need to come back for quite a while. With her in tow, he led the way out to his vehicle. He loaded her luggage in the bed of his truck and then, with a raised hand, said, "Let's go."

She got into the passenger seat without arguing. As he turned on his vehicle, he stared at her intently, watching for any signs. "I'm still taking you to my place."

She stiffened, then shrugged. She didn't say anything, and that pissed him off even more. "What's wrong?" he asked, trying hard to mask his frustration with her attitude.

"Everything, absolutely fucking everything." With that, she fell silent.

CHAPTER 5

P EARL NOTED GIDEON had stopped in a driveway.
"This is my house," he said, as he exited the vehicle
to get her bags.

Pearl looked around in surprise. *But he told me that he
didn't live here, didn't he?* Plus, the house was what they
would have bought together. They had talked about buying
something similar, and it almost brought tears to her eyes
when she realized that, in reality, he *had* bought their dream
home. The thing that stung the most was that he'd bought it
without her, all because she hadn't been here. She hadn't
been part of his dream anymore. She hadn't been part of any
of those plans because she wasn't a part of him anymore. It
was such an odd feeling to know that he'd gone ahead with
everything because it had mattered to him, whether she was
here or not.

His arms full, he nudged her to the front door.

As he dumped her bags into his spare room, he turned to
her. "I need you to stay inside. I'll come back in approxi-
mately … Give me an hour."

She gazed at him and then nodded.

"Please," he whispered, "don't run away."

Her eyebrows shot up, as she recognized her own wording. Then she nodded. "It's not as if I have my car anyway."

He gave her a bright smile. "Good point. I'll have it brought over for you, or we can go get it when I return. Right now I have to go talk to your bosses. So I need to know that you'll be here when I come back, and we can talk then."

She nodded.

"Help yourself to food, tea, whatever." And, with that, he was gone.

If she could have thought or guessed that this was how her day would end, she would have laughed herself silly. Absolutely no way this could have happened, even in her dreams. Yet here she was, moved into his house, yet not the way she had hoped.

She slowly walked around the house and explored it. It was beautiful, with three small bedrooms upstairs. Downstairs had a country kitchen and a big open living room with a huge fireplace and the master suite. The furniture was worn but comfortable, very much his style. She smiled as she collapsed on the big couch, wondering what she was supposed to do with her world now. Everything seemed so off, so wrong. Not that it was her fault at this point by any means, but it just didn't feel right. She wondered if anything would ever feel right again.

She still struggled with whatever the hell her coworker had stuffed into that jar. In her mind, she thought it was human waste, and yet she didn't know why or whose, not that she wanted to take a guess. She sat here for the longest time. When she heard a noise outside, she froze, then got up slowly and looked out the window. She couldn't see anything, but that didn't mean much.

She waited, and a couple more odd noises came, but

nothing she could pinpoint. Finally she went out into the backyard and still couldn't see anything. As she sat here waiting, she thought she saw a puppy, rough looking, half wet, crying, and digging at something in the very back. She walked over to the corner and realized that it must have got in under the rear fence. A spot was dug out just big enough for this little guy.

He took one look at her and immediately crouched down low in fear.

She murmured to him, "Hey, it's okay, buddy. I understand. I've been in a spot or two like this myself." She reached out to try and touch him, but he immediately backed off, crying with high-pitched yelps.

She sat here for a long time, just waiting for him to calm down. When she finally managed to get close enough to grab him, she picked him up and carried him into the house. He was hungry, cold, and appeared to be completely abandoned. No collar, nothing to say anybody gave a crap about him. But she cared. If nothing else, it was something she could do for somebody else, and, in her world, that was a huge help on a day like today.

Taking him in, she found a little bit of sliced meat, which probably wasn't the best for him, and a little bit of milk and some mixed veggies in the fridge. She mashed everything up, knowing it might probably hit his empty stomach like a rock, and gave him a few bites.

When he gobbled it up, she tentatively gave him a little bit more and a little bit more, not wanting to overstretch his stomach or to fill him up with food that might upset him. But he didn't seem to have any trouble getting anything to go down. When she thought he'd had enough, she gave him a little bit of milk to help wash it down. When he had trouble drinking that unknown substance, she gave him more water.

Then she picked him up and carried him into the bathroom, where she ran a small bath and quickly scrubbed him down using shampoo. When he was clean, she grabbed several towels, scrubbed him top to bottom to dry him as much as she could, and then took him out into the backyard to spend a few minutes to help him dry off.

Somehow she'd found another animal in need, and it did give her something other than herself to worry about. This was a perfect answer to her rotten day.

When her phone rang a little bit later, she caught it up, breathless. "Hello."

After a moment of silence on the other end, Gideon asked her, "Are you okay?"

"I'm fine." She laughed out loud. "You might not be when you get here, but, yes, I'm fine."

"You want to explain that?" he asked.

"No, I don't want to explain anything, just in case you don't like it," she replied. "You will see when you get here, and, if it's an issue for you, I'll find a way to fix it, no matter what." When no answer came, she laughed again. "I promise I didn't destroy your house."

"I couldn't care less about the house," he said, "but you do have me a bit worried."

"No, it's fine, … unless you don't like animals."

"Animals?" he repeated. "What on earth are you talking about? I just called to see if you wanted me to pick up some food."

"Did you talk to my bosses?"

"I sure did, at least one of them. I'll track down the other one."

"Have fun with that," she murmured. "Anyway, food would be good. You had some leftovers, but I may have just used up a bunch."

An odd note filled his tone as he asked, "You used up a bunch?"

"As I said, it's complicated."

"Doesn't sound very complicated at all. It sounds like something's been going on while I've been gone."

"Yes," she agreed immediately. "Something did go on while you weren't here, but I don't want to say anything because I don't want to give you something to get upset about before you get here." He groaned at that, and she added, "I'm not being mysterious."

"In that case you're failing," he countered immediately.

"Well, fine, pick up some dinner, and you'll see when you get here." With that, she ended the call and planned to go back to rubbing down the puppy. She found him curled up in the towel, sound asleep. As she picked him up, he gave several tiny whimpers. She hugged him close and whispered, "It's okay, buddy. Not sure who you belong to or where you came from, but at least your world has changed today."

He gave several more whimpers, as he snuggled in her arms, but she just relaxed inside on the couch and held him close. Within minutes, he fell asleep. She felt such a sense of peace, a sense of joy that he would trust her. She didn't know what the protocol was for an animal like this, since it was obvious that he didn't have a regular home or a place where anybody gave a crap because he didn't have any food or a collar.

Of course maybe he was lost, and somebody was out there looking for him. She hoped not because, as far as she was concerned, he was hers. If Pearl needed anything right now, it was somebody and something to love. Asking this little guy to love her back was probably too much at this point, but she would take anything the puppy had to give.

She woke with a start, unsure of where she was and what she heard. Hugging the puppy, she quickly oriented herself, recalling the events that led up to her being here in Gideon's house. She gradually became aware of the sounds that had woken her. She set the puppy gently on the couch, as she got up to investigate. A young family was spread out on the sidewalk, calling back and forth to each other, as they posted something on the utility poles.

With a sinking feeling, she realized what they could be doing. Her glance over at the sofa revealed the still sleeping little pup, clearly exhausted. With a reluctant look outside, she saw how fervently the children were working. Opening the door, she called out to the nearest one, a boy of around eight, and asked what they were doing. When he showed her the flyer he carried, the pain in her heart was immediately healed by the tremble in his chin. as he explained that they were missing their puppy, who had dug under their fence and was out overnight.

With a smile, she waved over the mother and told the boy to stay right here. Back inside, she took a moment to snuggle the clean, dry, and contented little pup, whispering her thanks for making her day a little brighter. Then she slipped outside to reunite him with his delighted family.

GIDEON QUICKLY DROVE to one of his favorite restaurants, picked up the takeout order he'd called in, his mind reeling, wondering what the hell Pearl had been up to. She'd only been at his place a few hours, and already something was up. Yet she sounded happier somehow, an element of joy in her tone, a sense of peace and relaxation that hadn't been there before. That was a good thing. If she hadn't destroyed anything, he was pretty sure he could live with whatever this was, and she may well need something because, as far as he was concerned, she desperately needed a new job.

He'd only managed to talk to her immediate supervisor, but Maria had explained quite a bit more about the antics that this Betty person had been up to. The manager had been nervous, saying she had reported it to her supervisors, but nobody ever did anything about it. Gideon had calls in to the next level supervisor, someone Maria seemed afraid of, likely because that person had the ability to make things happen, the potential fear that Pearl's job would be lost, even Maria's.

As far as Gideon was concerned, Pearl's job quite possibly needed to go anyway, especially if this was the crap going on in that place.

When he pulled into his driveway, his phone rang. He answered it to find Grant Hollick, the missing boss he'd been waiting to speak to. When Grant asked what the call was about, his tone was brisk, as if time were a serious issue, as if Gideon were completely disrupting him, saying he didn't have time for such nonsense.

"I see," Gideon replied. This guy wasn't interested in being helpful. "In that case, I'll see you down at the base for questioning tomorrow morning."

Dead silence came on the other end. "What are you talking about?" he asked too quickly. "I'm a busy man here. I don't have time for these games."

"No? Apparently you don't have time to look after your

employees either, and now it's gone past anybody hiding anything," Gideon declared. "So I will see you at the base tomorrow morning. Nine o'clock sharp, please."

"I can't meet at nine. I have an appointment."

"I suggest you change that appointment," Gideon stated, his tone inflexible. "I will see you there in the morning. Otherwise, we can send an MP car to pick you up."

"I'm hardly a criminal, young man. Do you know who you're talking to?"

"Yes, I do. I left a message for you to call me, remember?"

CHAPTER 6

AFTER PEARL AND Gideon ate, she quickly cleaned the kitchen and looked over at him. "I don't know whether that was lunch or dinner," she said in a half-joking manner.

"It's close enough to dinner that we'll call it a done deal. If you're hungry later, there's always leftovers," he suggested. "As long as you haven't fed them to a stray by then."

Smiling at the joke, she replied, "Thanks for being a good sport about that. A puppy is the last thing we need to be dealing with, but it seemed like the thing to do at the time."

"In light of the circumstances, it probably worked out for the best," Gideon conceded. "I did tell you to make yourself at home."

"Thanks." She hesitated and added meekly, "Would you mind if I had a shower and just called it a night?"

He nodded. "That's fine, as long as you're not running away."

Heat flushed through her face, immediately draining away everything inside her. She sagged into the kitchen chair, just staring at him, wordless.

He sat down across from her and picked up her hands. "I'm sorry. That was a cheap shot."

"No," she whispered, "I deserved it."

He shook his head. "You can stop that talk anytime," he muttered. "It's not about you."

"It might be about me now." She shook her head. "I feel like I'm ..." Then she laughed and just left it at that. She was not sure how to say anything right now. "It's always about me, isn't it?" she muttered, with a moan. "It's not supposed to be that way, and honestly, it's not about me. It's about us. It's about who I should be, not who I am."

"And again, that's not the person you were," he stated, staring at her oddly.

"Yeah, ... well, five years of realizing I walked away from something I wanted to keep does that to me. It hasn't been an easy thing to come to terms with. I have blamed myself time and time again for my actions."

"So why didn't you reach out in all that time?" he asked. "Why not make a call or send me a text, anything just to say, *Hey, I'm alive.* I've been away a lot on various assignments, but my base has always been here at Coronado."

"I did try the base, until I realized you'd left. Then I just saw a closed door in front of me." She glanced over at him, a corner of her mouth tilting upward. It was all she could manage in the form of a smile. "Think about how you would feel if you ever did anything embarrassing like that. At the time, I hadn't realized that I was running away," she noted, with a shrug. "I did check on your status a couple times but discovered you were out of the country again, so that was that."

"I guess I can understand to some degree," he murmured. "I just wish that you had reached out, mostly because it was hell not knowing if you were okay. It was hell knowing that you had completely washed me out of your life after what? After five years together?"

"Five years together, then five years apart," she whispered, with a nod. "It seems so surreal to even see you seated across from me right now."

He shook his head, got up, and walked around. "I don't know about surreal, but I'm definitely having some trouble adapting."

She smiled. "Yet you're the one who was always good at adapting to situations." She felt the brunt of everything hitting her at the same time. "It's why you're so good at what you do," she murmured. "You have always been good at quickly adjusting."

"You think so?" he asked, with a half laugh. "For the record, I didn't adapt very well after you left. Not with no explanation, nothing more than just a sudden, *Hey, I need something new in my life*, or whatever you told me."

Her breath sucked back and froze in her chest for a long moment, before she managed to release the pain inside along with her pent-up breath. "I'm sorry."

He glared at her. "*Sorry?* Fuck the whole *I'm sorry* part," he spat, "because, in case you hadn't noticed, I still harbor a hell of a lot of anger inside me."

"I can see that," she acknowledged, without moving, staring at him like a hawk.

He groaned as he sat down, she could see he was holding back the onslaught of everything he had kept buried for so long, boiling under the surface all the time. "The thing about my anger is that it masks something else," he admitted, "and, in this case, fear. Fear that I'd lost you, fear that you were gone from my life forever. Fear that you had some disease, that you had another lover, that you had something I didn't know about. You were closed off to the point that I couldn't even reach you. I didn't even know what the problem was, and it happened so fast. My mind went from a cancer diagnosis to a new love to sudden depression, and I couldn't figure it out."

She shook her head. "Can we just say I was having a moment?"

"Yeah, a five-year moment," he noted in a deadpan tone.

For the first time—in between all the drama of the day—the humor of it struck her, and she laughed. "Yes, I guess that's one way to look at it."

"That's true," he muttered, as he tried to relax into his seat. "So, where do we go from here?"

"I don't know. ... Is there anywhere to go?" She looked around, then winced at the audacity of it all. "I'm in your house, having called you, begging for help." She shook her head. "I had no idea who else to turn to. You were automatically the one person I called out for, when I was scared and in trouble."

"That's a good thing," he said, his tone very gentle. "Of all of the people you know, I'm one of the few who deals in this stuff."

"What was *this stuff* anyway?" she asked. "It makes no sense. Why would that guy be in my house?"

"He was waiting for you, but again it had more to do with your location."

She stared at him, recalling that he had mentioned it before, but she wasn't getting anything new from what he was saying.

"Do you know your neighbors?" he asked.

"My neighbors?" she repeated, then turned back to him. "We already went over this."

"Do you know what they drive? Do you remember if

they put the garbage out on a regular basis? Do you know if they get a lot of visitors? Do you know anything about them at all?"

She immediately shook her head. "No, I don't. Honestly, I work hard, come home, and then, with all the extra BS at work, my home is where I just hide away," she explained, speaking too slowly for him. "I've hardly even gone out for anything." She shrugged her shoulders. "Of course after my parents died, that just made it all worse."

"Wait, what? Your parents died?" he asked, staring at her in shock.

She winced. She hadn't even left him so much as a message about that. "Yeah, a few months after I left. A car accident."

"Good God." He stared at her. "You loved your parents."

"I did, and still do in many ways," she replied, with a smile. "Obviously they're dead, and their passing was one of those major turning points in life. So, on top of losing you— though that was my own fault—then I lost them. ... I was lost in a big way."

He grasped her hands. "I'm sorry, sweetheart. I wish you had told me."

"I do too. Seriously, I do because I felt incredibly isolated from the world at that point. They were all I had. We had some issues with the estate that took me a bit to sort out, plus issues with the lawyer. We didn't have the new will supposedly, and that was just one more of the things that seem so trivial now. Still, at the time, it was hard to get through," she murmured.

"What was the issue?"

"My parents had told me very specifically that they

wanted to be cremated, but their will that the lawyer had said something completely different. So I had to fight the lawyer about it. He wanted to handle everything himself, and he fought for control. Of course he was a good friend of theirs."

"Of course, but that doesn't make it any easier, does it?"

"No, not at all. I'm glad I had the last six months with them. I would like to think that I had some foreknowledge that it would all happen, and that's why I went home," she shared, "but that's not true. I didn't have any way to know. If I had known, I absolutely would have come home, and who knows? Maybe I wouldn't have cut you out."

"No way to know at this point," Gideon noted. "Anyway, let's not keep going back over the same issues. So, did you have them dealt with the way you wanted to?"

She nodded. "I did, finally. It wasn't fun or pleasant, but then I also had to sell their house. It was never my house to begin with, as you recall." She snorted. "It never felt like home to me, and I never lived there, so it was very much their place. I didn't want to live back East or keep the house, but selling it—although it didn't take all that long—was still a long time."

She took a moment to collect herself. "The process of cleaning out the house was pretty horrific at the end of the day," she shared. "I spent that first year, year and a half, just dealing with things pertaining to my parents that had to be dealt with. By the time I lifted my head, even more time had gone by, and I just didn't know how to go back."

"Yet you're here."

"I'm here. After everything was sold, I ended up with a job in one of the hospitals, and it was fine, but I didn't feel like I had a real purpose. Eventually I started seeing a therapist." She gave him a mocking smile. "I didn't know I needed it, but I am forever grateful to the woman who helped me get my head on straight. At that point in time, I wasn't sure what *straight* even looked like." She gave a small laugh. "It's amazing how screwed up you can be and not even know it."

"I think it happens to a lot of people, particularly after some major life changes like that."

She nodded. "That's basically what happened to me. Anyway, through it all, I realized that, of all the things I regretted, the biggest mistake I made was walking away from you," she admitted, with a smile and a straight face. "My therapist always wanted me to come back and talk to you."

"Which would have been a sensible decision," he added.

"Sure, but it had already been years by then—three, I think. We were into the third year by that point in time, and I didn't know how to make that happen. When a job came up here about six months later, I applied for it, and it was another six months or so before I heard from them, got the job, and signed back up again." She smiled. "Then suddenly I found myself here, only to find out that you were not." She sighed, remembering just how much of a shock that had been, something she still struggled to accept.

"So, you didn't do any research before you came back?"

She looked over at him and shook her head. "None. For some reason I just assumed that the man I had always been the happiest with would have stayed here."

"Maybe. Except the man who was always the happiest here had lost the one thing that made him happy. So this no longer felt like home. It just became a place. I tried to make it mine, even getting this house, but it still never felt quite right. When I got an opportunity to go overseas, I took it. I needed the change and something else to look at, like a new view on life," he shared. "I popped in and out of here occasionally, checking on the house and all. Sometimes I rented it out to guys for short-term stays here and there, so it didn't just sit here vacant."

She nodded. "Did you ever find anybody else?" she asked, hating that the question half choked her up.

He immediately shook his head. "Not on a long-term basis. I tried a couple relationships, but I was still hurting," he replied, "and trust was a big issue."

"*Right*, I can understand that."

"Can you?" he asked intently. "When you did what you did for no reason, it messed with my head. Every imaginable excuse came to me, but absolutely none of them made any sense. I couldn't make heads or tails out of it. So, I tended to look at every relationship after that as being short-term because there probably wouldn't ever be anything long-term." She winced, opened her mouth, and he immediately squeezed her fingers. "Don't you dare say you're sorry."

Her shoulders slumped, as she nodded. "And yet I am. It was one thing to hurt myself through all this. It was quite another to hurt you."

He burst out laughing. "I am hardly innocent in all this." He shook his head. "I could have reached out to you. I could have actively tried to figure out what was going on. I am an investigator, after all. I could have tried harder to stay in touch. Let's face it. I could have done a million things, but instead I let you go. Mostly because I was hurting and confused. I just didn't understand, so I kept on hiding."

Surprised, she raised an eyebrow at the phrase.

He nodded. "That's what happens when people get hurt. We go inside and just hide because it feels better than not hiding. We don't want anybody to ask questions, and we sure as hell don't want to explain it to anybody. Hell, I didn't have any explanation."

"I understand that too."

"What could I say to people? *Yeah, she just walked out. No, I have no idea why.* Everybody would have just laughed me off the street, and yet it was the truth."

"Yes, it was," she muttered, and then she groaned. "Life's a mess, isn't it?"

"It certainly can be." Just then his phone rang. He got up and answered it, then took one look at her and pointed behind him. "I have to take this in the other room."

She nodded and watched as he walked away. She stared around the kitchen, wondering at his need to talk, versus letting her run off to bed. Running away to her room would have been easier. Yet, at this moment, she was glad that he had encouraged her to stay, and together they confronted the elephant in the room. It was a little easier to talk to him now, though she didn't expect it to make things easier in the long term. Still, anything that made it easier in the short term was a blessing.

When he rejoined her, a frown evident on his face, she got worried. "What's up?"

"I've got to step out," he said.

"Okay, go." She gave a wave of her hand. "You don't need to babysit me."

He laughed. "That's partly why you're here. You know that, right?"

"What? So you can watch over me?"

"Yes. The gunman was at your house, and we don't yet know if he had an ulterior motive for choosing your house versus another house or whether somebody is worried that they were seen or that *you* saw something."

"I don't have the slightest idea what any of this is all about in the first place," she replied. "So, you do you, but I don't see how your leaving the house is an issue."

"Lock up behind me, and we'll have a black-and-white unit cruise by several times and check up on you."

She stared at him. "I gather you'll be gone a long time?"

"I have no idea," he answered honestly, "but sometimes, when I have to go, I have to go for a while."

"Right." She nodded. "I plan on going to bed and getting some rest anyway. So anything that you need to do, go do it," she said. "I'm not here to hold you back in any way. So please continue to work as you've always worked."

He laughed. "That'll be a little hard to do when you're sitting here in my house after all these years."

"Right, but it's not as if anything has changed."

He stared at her, his face grim. "And that's enough of that BS too," he declared, with an intense searching gaze, "because the truth is, everything has changed."

CHAPTER 7

A S SOON AS Gideon left, Pearl locked the door behind him and headed upstairs, where she took a shower, changed, and slipped into bed. It felt so strange to be in this house. It wasn't hers; it was his. Yet it was everything they'd always talked about having together. She lay here stiff under the covers, wondering not only at her nervousness, but also the strangeness of it all. Just as she drifted off, she thought she heard the door downstairs. She waited, thinking it was likely him. She picked up her phone and sent him a quick text, asking if it was. Almost immediately she got a response right back.

No. What are you hearing?

Frowning, she slipped out of bed and walked to the door and listened. Hearing footsteps on the stairs, she immediately texted him back. **Footsteps, somebody coming up the stairs.** She felt the panic building inside because, if it wasn't him, who the hell was it?

Instead of phoning her, he texted. **Open the window on the side. A small deck is there. Close the window behind you. A tree is nearby. Step out onto it.**

She stared down at her phone, shaking her head. No way she ever considered that. But hearing another footstep coming up the stairs—stealthy, stopping at every squeak—she raced to the window and realized that he was right. A small balcony was here, little more than a ledge, but she stepped out onto it wishing she had better footwear than slippers. She closed the window, so, if somebody did come into her room, they wouldn't know she'd gone out this way. Then she stepped around to the side of the house and saw the tree that he was talking about.

A huge branch was right here, and she immediately climbed onto it and hid up in the tree. Although, if somebody had a flashlight and shone it in her direction, it would be hard for her to stay hidden. So she climbed higher up in the tree, feeling the wind whip around and past her, wondering what the hell she was doing and how the hell she'd ended up climbing out a second-story window into a tree in her pajamas at this hour.

Her phone kept buzzing, and, by the time she was in a safe position, she found at least a dozen text messages from Gideon. She sent one back. **I made it into the tree.**

She immediately got a thumbs-up.

On the way was the second message she got, right after that.

She sighed with relief, then leaned her head back against the trunk, and when nobody looked out her bedroom window, when nobody came to the window at all or was even outside the house, she had to wonder.

Had she just imagined all this? Would Gideon come home and find the house vacant, with no evidence of an intruder, and her sitting in the tree, wondering at her overactive imagination?

Hearing vehicles coming up the road, she froze, looking to see if it was him. All she wanted was for Gideon to come home and rescue her. Even the thought made her wince because, damn, since when had she become someone who needed rescuing? Particularly by Gideon specifically. But while she had hidden higher up in the tree, it occurred to her that she might have been hidden enough that the intruder couldn't see her, and she may not see him either. But she did have a good view of the vehicle out front, and she saw somebody dash out of the house and get into that vehicle.

He didn't look like he had anything with him. She immediately texted Gideon, saying a vehicle out front was picking up the intruder. She got a thumbs-up back immediately, and suddenly another vehicle came roaring up behind the one that was in the front. The intruder's vehicle took off, and the second one gave chase. Moments later, two more cars came screeching up and parked at the house.

Immediately she saw someone she thought could be Jasper, while the occupants from the other vehicle all converged at the base of the tree. Jasper called out, "Pearl, you still up there?"

Peering through the leaves, she recognized him, and two military police were with him, easily recognizable by their uniforms. "Yes," she called out. "You want to check out the house and make sure that he didn't come with somebody else?"

"These two guys will go in and do that," Jasper replied. "I want you to come down."

"That's nice," she said, with a shaky laugh, "but I'm not quite sure how to get down."

He let out a bark of laughter. "Yet you got up there."

"Not exactly," she replied, with a shrieking tone. "I crawled out the window onto the balcony, then onto the tree."

"Can you go back that same way?"

She hesitated, then maneuvered herself over to the big branch and stared at it, but it looked a whole lot different now that she wasn't motivated by someone coming after her. "Maybe," she murmured, "but I'm not completely sure."

"Okay, don't worry about it. I'll come up to the bedroom and help you get back that way. Just stay right there."

She waited a few minutes, then suddenly Jasper was there, opening the big window to the bedroom.

He smiled at her. "That's a hell of a system."

"Not what I expected. When I called Gideon and told him somebody was in the house, he immediately told me to step out on the balcony and into the tree."

Jasper nodded at that. "I'm not surprised to find that Gideon has escape routes prepared for his home." Jasper laughed. "Obviously he knew this one was here and would work for you. Can you climb back over onto the balcony ledge or do you want me to come to you?"

She stared down at the ground, looked over at him, and whispered, "Maybe I can make it to you."

He hopped out onto the ledge, got over to the big branch, and held out his arms, urging her forward, "Just come slow. Once you've got my hand, we've got it made."

"Not if I fall," she pointed out. "I'll just take you down with me."

He laughed. "Don't you worry about that. I've got you."

Sure enough, as soon as she made her way halfway across the branch, her knees shaking, her breath raspy in her throat, she reached out, and there he was. Jasper grabbed her hand and got her back onto the balcony, then in through the window.

He took a good look around and said, "That's a hell of a

deal."

"And yet, if you think about it, it could also let some-body into the house. Somebody taller than me, I guess."

"I'm sure Gideon was focusing on escape routes. Either way, these things always have pros and cons." He smiled and patted her on the shoulder. "Come on. Let's get you down-stairs and start a cup of tea or something."

She followed him downstairs, grateful when she saw the two military police standing at the front door. "I gather nobody is in the house?" she asked them, and they both shook their heads but didn't say a word. "I told Gideon that somebody picked up one intruder who came out, using that side door." She pointed in that direction. Immediately one of the MPs headed in that direction. "That's when a vehicle came up behind and took off after them."

"The vehicle that came up behind and took off was Gid-eon," Jasper confirmed, with a smile. "He's still giving chase right now."

"Oh," she whispered, just staring. "That's not safe though, is it?"

"I wouldn't worry about that. Gideon knows what he's doing."

She nodded blankly and sat where Jasper pointed. "I didn't think this day could get any stranger. Yet moments ago I'm sitting outside, up in a tree at Gideon's house—a house that perfectly represents the home we had always daydreamed about buying together." She shook her head, shaking away the nostalgia. "It's surreal." She looked around the kitchen, her arms wrapped around her chest. "This is not exactly how I thought my day would go."

"No, I'm sure it's not. What can you tell me about this Betty person?"

Startled, she looked over at him and shrugged. "She hates me for some reason, and that's all I can tell you. She insults me, talks down to me, says nasty things about me to other staff members and even to our patients. It's been so blatant that I don't even know how or why she's still there," she added. "My direct supervisor has taken action numerous times, but it seems like somebody higher up is protecting her."

"One of those bosses is scheduled to come to the base in the morning," Jasper told her, with a smile, "so we'll ask him about that."

"Will they come? The bosses, I mean."

"Yeah, it's been arranged. Gideon can be very persuasive when he wants to be. So, what kind of person is Betty? Is she particularly beautiful? Is she the kind to have affairs at work?"

Pearl started at Jasper, then shrugged. "Honestly, I don't know about that. I've only ever seen the nasty side of her, so it's hard for me to envision anybody wanting anything to do with her."

"Got it. Anyway, we should get more answers tomorrow."

"I don't think you'll get any answers at all. I think whoever is out there will continue to protect her."

"Maybe so," Jasper conceded, "but, either way, we'll get some of the information we need."

"What about the dead guy, the intruder at my house?"

"We were able to identify him. Have you ever heard of anybody named Larry Darwill?"

"Darwill," she repeated and shook her head. "No."

"That's fine. We'll do a full workup now that we're getting somewhere."

"Somewhere?" she asked, with a faint look in his direction. "As far as I'm concerned, we're nowhere. Nowhere at all. For some reason they thought they needed to break into my house and now Gideon's house."

"I get that, and, back at your house, we're studying everything your windows look out on to see which property, which house, might possibly interest them."

"Gideon mentioned something about that to me earlier, asking if I'd noticed anything about my neighbors, who might have strange visitors and all that stuff," she shared, "but I have no clue. I don't watch the neighbors or their visitors. I generally come home tired, worn out, and fed up. I get quite depressed and turn in early, only to start it all over again." She was aware that he was staring at her. She shrugged. "Yeah, not exactly healthy."

"It's more than just not healthy," he noted. "Depression is a serious issue."

"I don't know that I'm depressed as much as confused, worn out, and upset at the choices I made."

"By choices, you mean, walking away from Gideon?"

She nodded. "Did he tell you about that?"

"No. … He didn't have to. It's evident that whatever went on between you two, you're either regretting it or somehow wishing you could change things in some way."

"That's true," she murmured. "I walked away from him quite a few years ago. I still don't have a good idea why, except that I was panicked at the idea of him proposing," she admitted, with a laugh. "Yet that's what we talked about. We talked about it all the time. Then, when push came to shove, I just panicked," she murmured. "I took off and left him hanging, with no good explanation, so he hates me now."

"Gideon?" he asked, turning to look at her.

She lifted her gaze and nodded. "Yeah, why wouldn't he?"

"Because he's not the guy who wastes much time with things like hate. He's one of the good guys in the world." Then he laughed. "If anything, he would bend over backward to try and make your world happy."

"Maybe," she murmured, "but I screwed up, and generally, when you screw up, you pay the price."

"And sometimes"—Jasper walked over and sat at the opposite side of the table—"sometimes the price isn't as high as we think it'll be."

She stared at him in confusion. "Are you telling me that I don't deserve to have him walk away from me?"

"Did you tell him that you were looking to get back together? Or did you just assume that he understood?"

She frowned, then shrugged. "I don't think we ever got that far. It's been a pretty confusing time."

He burst out laughing at that. "I won't argue with you on that. This has all the makings of one of the strangest scenarios I've had to deal with in a very long time."

"Aren't you here for a friend of yours?"

"I'm here for Tesla, who is technically my cousin, but more like a sister to me," he shared. "Her husband, Mason, was recently shot on base."

"Oh, of course, I heard about that," she said, as she stared at him. "That's quite a feat in itself." His eyebrows shot up, and she shrugged. "The base is pretty secure, and everybody has weapons already, so why would you shoot somebody when you're taking the chance of getting your own ass shot?"

He stared at her for a long moment, then slowly smiled. "I like that. Somebody who can think, somebody who's not so quick to judge what's going on with an explanation that doesn't make a whole lot of sense. The thing is, we don't know what happened yet or why. We just know that a sniper atop a building took Mason out, while he was getting off an airplane. He had just landed on base, saw his wife a distance away, turned to walk toward her, then *boom*. He went down."

"So was the shooter trying to show Mason how everything he wanted in life could be taken away? Then there's his wife ..."

"Pregnant wife at that," Jasper interrupted.

Pearl nodded. "So, everything Mason wants in the world, his wife, his child, a happy homecoming waiting for him, and, in a split second, somebody takes it all away. It would be a good revenge move, if somebody felt that's what happened to them."

Gideon walked in just then, and he stopped at the doorway, hearing her words. "I always appreciated that about you," he murmured.

She got up and hesitated, as he opened his arms. She tried to hold back a sob, but part of it escaped as she ran over to the security provided by his arms, which he wrapped around her. "I don't know what you could possibly have appreciated," she murmured.

"Your brain," he said. "You seek connections that other people don't see." He led her back to the table and sat her down again. He looked over at Jasper. "What do you think of her theory?"

Jasper turned to him and nodded. "I hadn't considered anything that specific. We've talked about revenge as a motive but not in such a deliberate way."

"The other thing you should do is twist that around,"

Pearl suggested. "What if the bullet was directed at his wife?"

"How so?"

"Maybe there is some event in her past that you need to look at, and, instead of your friend Mason being the one who sees everything taken from him, it's her."

GIDEON HAD ALREADY been through the whole gambit of emotions today, even seeing her in his kitchen, where he always imagined seeing her, in their home, which just felt so right. Meanwhile, something was so wrong about a car chase, where unfortunately the intruder and his driver were in a street car and managed to pull away from his rental truck, to the point that he hadn't been able to keep up behind them. He'd lost them somewhere in the shopping mall. Although now a full alert would be placed on the vehicle, it wouldn't be long before they found the car. Yet he hadn't found the intruder himself.

He had a security system here at this house, and he would have a look at that. In the meantime, just hearing her theories and watching Jasper reassessing them, made Gideon smile. He looked over at Jasper to see his take. "She always did have the ability to confound me with things like that. She sees patterns and synchronicity that I never did."

She looked over at him and shrugged. "The shooter sees everything get taken away from him. Then, as Tesla, I'm waiting for Mason's plane to land. I'm pregnant. The father of my child is on his way home. Obviously they love each other, and, in that split second, *poof.* He's gone. Isn't that important too?"

"It's very important," Jasper noted, as he slowly stood

up. He looked over at Gideon. "I think I'll head to the office."

"Not to Tesla?"

"No, it's too late to talk to Tesla," he said, with the wave of his hand, "but I will send her a text, and, if she's still awake, I'll call her."

"I'll check out my security cameras, and I'll send you whatever I can find."

"You do that," Jasper replied, his tone thoughtful as he turned and walked out.

Gideon made tea for her and then added, "I'll check on my security system tapes to see who came into the house and how he got in."

"Oh, good, I wasn't sure if you had something like that."

He snorted. "Of course I do," he murmured. "This is me after all."

"I'm glad to see some things haven't changed," she murmured. "I was trying to figure out how he got into the house at all."

"That's one of the things I need to look at. You can come along, if you want." Together, with her carrying her tea, he led her to a small room he had set up with a laptop and several monitors, so he could see all angles of the property.

"Wow," she murmured, "this is great." He turned on a couple other monitors, and then she realized cameras were inside the house as well. "Interesting." She stared at the screens. "I didn't realize I was being watched."

"You weren't. You were being recorded. That's different."

"The difference is minute, but I get how it makes a difference to you." Once he tapped into the right time frame, he showed her walking through the living room and heading upstairs. The camera followed until she went into her bedroom, and then it stopped.

"Thank God for that," she muttered.

He cracked a smile in her direction. "A camera is in there, but I turned it off when I got it ready for you."

She nodded. "Is it necessary?"

"It is necessary," he replied, in all seriousness, and then he clicked on another camera view, outside her bedroom. He sucked in his breath as he watched her very carefully go out on that tree branch.

"That wasn't exactly a shining moment in my life," she murmured. "I was pretty terrified out there."

"Are you kidding? That was definitely a shining moment in your life." He turned and gave her a brilliant smile that made her heart warm.

She chuckled, as she sat down beside him.

"You got yourself out of a bad situation. You stayed calm. You followed instructions. You got to safety, and that asshole didn't find you."

"Do you think he was looking for me?" she murmured.

"I don't know. That'll be the first question." He flicked through a bunch of other cameras and took the video back to when he had left the house. About fifteen minutes from the time that he walked outside and drove away, another vehicle dropped off a solo male, who then approached the house, walked around to the side, and, under full view of the cameras, used a key and let himself in. Gideon whistled at that. "I'll definitely have to change the locks."

"How the hell?" she whispered.

"I don't know, but I'll find out."

As the video played, she just stared, her jaw dropping as

he walked through the house, almost as if he knew where he was going. As he got to the stairs, he turned, looked around, and then slowly, ever-so-slowly, climbed the stairs.

"See his movements there?" he asked.

She nodded.

Gideon continued. "He knew you were here. Otherwise he absolutely had no reason to approach those stairs."

"Particularly, if he already knew that they squeak."

He glanced at her and nodded.

She added, "Which means he's been in your house before."

"Yeah, I got that message all right," he snorted. "Whether it was a reconnaissance mission or he was just looking for trouble, I don't know," he murmured.

He flicked through several more camera angles and got a picture of the man's face. He wore a baseball cap, and it was pulled down low, and he seemed to avoid looking at the cameras—though that may not have been intentional as much as he was focused on what he was doing.

Finally, upstairs when he got to the hallway, he turned to look at the rooms, and the camera caught his face, not full-on because of the hat but the bottom part of his jaw. Immediately Gideon backtracked the video, slowed it down, then took several screenshots of the man's face. "It's not the whole face, but it's something."

She leaned forward and then pointed out, "Look at that."

"Look at what?"

"His hand," she said. "Look at the back of his hand there."

Gideon went through the other videos, looking to see if they got any other view. Only when he placed his hand on the railing and his shirt sleeve pulled up was anything visible. Sure enough, something was on the back of his hand higher up on the wrist above the glove trim.

"A tattoo?" she asked.

"Maybe," he murmured, "let me see if I can get a better picture of it." He changed the video screens several times, going closer and expanding it back out again, until he got the best image that he could, and then he continued to play the security tape. The man froze, when he heard a sound coming from the spare room.

"That," Pearl noted, "was probably me getting out onto the branch. I had no idea it made so much noise."

"It's hard to prevent it," Gideon said. "You do what you can, but, when you think about it, you've got to open the window and climb out. It's not that easy to lift up your body mass onto the tree, especially if you're in a panic."

"I was definitely in a panic," she admitted, "something I'm not particularly proud of either."

He looked over at her and shook his head. "Stop being so hard on yourself," he scolded. "Think about it. Look at how much you've handled today. I think you've done amazingly well."

She beamed at him, and he realized just how little positivity must have been in her world lately, since just a simple compliment had settled her right back down again and put a pretty smile on her face. He smiled. "Honest to God, you've done amazingly well today, not to mention saving the puppy. By the way, I will be checking out the video on that later."

After they shared a laugh, he went back to searching for a better image and then finally sat back. "It doesn't look like we'll get a better picture of the back of his hand, and the gloves cover the fingers," he murmured.

"Can you do a search for that image somehow?"

"I can, and we will at work. They have better equipment there. I will also get the techs on this and see if they can tweak the image and get something more detailed."

"It would be great if you could because that would be huge for identifying this intruder," she shared, leaning forward as the guy crept down the stairs. "Something's off about his walk."

"I noticed," he murmured.

"It's almost as if one leg is either injured or shorter than the other one," she pointed out. "He's walking with an odd gait." She pointed to the screen. "Look at that. See that right there? He's hitching his leg. It's not that it doesn't work properly, but it doesn't have much of a lift in there, which would help to equalize the length of his legs. He's not off by much, just a little bit," she murmured. As the intruder reached for the door, she pointed at the screen. "See that?"

"Yeah," Gideon said, now watching how engaged and confident she had suddenly become.

"He twitched as he pulled open the door, so he's dealing with an injury of some kind. Like something is hurting his back just doing that little bit of a motion. He may have left because he wasn't sure he could handle a confrontation. I'm not sure what he came in for, but I don't think he's in fighting form." Gideon stared at her in amazement, as she shrugged. "Remember the work that I do?" she said, with a mock smile.

"I'd forgotten, but I won't forget it again." He quickly sent videos to the main office, sending them directly to Jasper. "Now, how about getting some sleep because tomorrow is likely to be quite busy."

"Is it safe to go to sleep?" she asked. "Somebody out there has keys to your house."

"Good point," he murmured, "but don't worry. We have ways of stopping doors from opening."

She followed him downstairs as he got 2x4s and propped them underneath the doorknobs so the doors couldn't be pushed open. "Nobody will come through this or push this open without waking me up."

She winced at that. "I would prefer if you just said that *nobody* would get in."

"I'm not somebody who will lie to you," he stated, with an odd smile. "In reality, somebody could get in, but they'll have a hell of a fight doing it. It would create quite a noise, a noise that he'll be fully aware that I'll hear."

"Right, so that will send you running, and, in theory, him running away."

"Exactly," he agreed. "So, let's get you back up to bed, and, with any luck, you can grab some sleep. I need to be at the office early anyway."

"Right. Can I come?" she asked.

"To the office?"

She nodded. "Honestly, I can't say I like the idea of staying here alone tomorrow, especially knowing that somebody has keys to your house."

"The locks will be changed pretty damn soon, but I get your meaning," he muttered. "Let's talk about it in the morning."

And, with that, he escorted her back to her room, checked to make sure it was empty and secure. Then headed to his own room. It would be a short night, and he needed whatever sleep he could get.

CHAPTER 8

PEARL WOKE UP the next morning to Gideon shaking her shoulder. When she bolted upright, he whispered, "Easy, easy, it's all right."

She looked around, half wild, and asked, "So what's going on?"

"It's eight o'clock already." He smiled. "I need to get to the office. I didn't want to just leave you alone and have you wake up to an empty house."

"Right." She groaned, collapsing onto the mattress to stare up at him, "I guess I wouldn't have appreciated that."

"I didn't think so," he said cheerfully. "If you want to come on down, we can get you a quick breakfast before we go."

"We?" she repeated, looking up at him, and then blinked. "Does that mean I can come to the office with you?"

"I don't think it's a bad idea, at least until we get some of this straightened out." He smiled again. "Get dressed, and I'll get the pancakes on."

The reminder of his pancakes sent a wave of homesickness through her. She nodded. "I'll be ready in just a minute."

He walked out, and she sat here on the bed for a long moment. Every Sunday they used to have pancakes, the two of them, just like they were all alone in the world. They spent the morning making love, and then they would get up on their own time, and he would always make pancakes. It was a memory she'd struggled with on Sundays for a very long time, until she'd finally managed to push it out of her mind and into the deep recesses of her history, where she would never go again. So to walk down there to his pancakes today would both be delicious and heartbreaking.

Determined to manage this emotional moment, she quickly dressed and walked downstairs, with a bright smile on her face. "You always did make the best pancakes."

"Ha, I don't know about the best, but they've always been a favorite food of mine."

She nodded at that, remembering that was why he made the pancakes. She was less of a pancake lover, but he made such great ones that she quickly became a fan. She sat down at the table, realizing it was already set and ready for her. "Any idea how long we'll be gone today?" she asked.

"Nope, I don't know, but the locks are getting changed at ten o'clock this morning," he shared, "and it will be done by somebody skilled." When she looked up at him, he nodded. "He's a former SEAL, but he's still around quite a bit."

"Is there such a thing as a former SEAL?"

Gideon smiled. "Let's just say, he's no longer active, but he's a good friend of Mason's, and he's hanging around, taking shifts on security when he can."

"I don't imagine there's any shortage of people wanting to help out with the security if a friend of theirs was shot."

"No, we don't have any problems with that," he agreed.

"On the other hand, sometimes too many people just complicate things too." She winced, but just then a plate of pancakes landed in front of her. "Enjoy."

"Wow," she murmured.

"I figured it could help get us both off to a good start today."

"I hope so," she muttered, as she quickly spread butter on top, added maple syrup, and cut into the stack. Taking her first bite, she sat back and stared at him, almost with tears in her eyes. He raised his eyebrows at her reaction. She just shrugged. "It's nothing."

"Obviously it's something."

She shrugged. "It's the pancakes. Lots of memories."

"Yeah." He stared down at the pancakes. "It's one of the reasons I kept making them. It brought back memories I didn't want to lose."

She didn't say anything to that, but her heart swelled with happiness at the thought that maybe still something was here for the two of them.

By the time they finished cleaning up the kitchen, he was rushing her to get out, so he made it to work in time. "Oh, yeah, you're interviewing one of my bosses."

Once they arrived, he was all business. "I want you to sit over on that side." He pointed off to a small area with chairs in it. "I'll be back in about half an hour, forty-five minutes. If anybody comes to talk to you, just tell them flat-out that you're not allowed to talk to anybody. That's it. No explanations, no feeling guilty, nothing."

Not sure what he was talking about, she just nodded, and he quickly disappeared into one of the offices.

When raised voices could be heard not very much later, she winced, wondering what the hell was going on. It wasn't long before the door slammed open, and somebody stepped out, his gaze furious, as he searched the outer rooms. When his gaze landed on her, he sucked back his breath and glared. "You," he snarled.

She immediately recognized one of the bosses at her work. She stared at him, not sure what was going on or why he was angry at her, but nothing in his world ever seemed to matter except him. She just remembered Gideon's warning and stayed quiet.

Her boss marched over in front of her. "If you think you'll have a job at the end of this," he snapped, snarling and biting his lips, "you're wrong. No way in hell I'll have you back there."

She caught sight of Gideon coming up behind him. When he arrived, he asked Pearl, "Are you okay?"

She nodded but didn't say anything. The other man, she thought his name was Grant, though she wasn't sure of the last name, continued to snarl. "This woman has been nothing but trouble," he snapped. "She'll get her ass fired right now."

"You won't fire her right now," Jasper declared, coming out of the other office. "We currently have a full investigation underway, and, for the moment, your authority has been revoked."

"What do you mean, revoked? I hold a much higher rank than you guys ever will, looking at the way you are doing things here." He was as furious as a raging storm and raising complete hell. "Just wait until I get my hands on your files."

At that, an official stepped into the room that she didn't know, but it made her boss's face turn pale. He immediately stood and saluted in greeting. "Sir, I didn't see you there."

"No, you didn't see me," the uniformed man confirmed, with a clipped nod, "but I was sitting in on the interview, watching you."

Grant's eyebrows shot up. "Sir?" he asked, with a confused look on his face. The initial storm had subsided, and just confusion remained now.

"You see, the woman, Betty, whom you've been protecting this entire time, the one who's been harassing her coworker," he explained, with a head tilt toward Pearl, "doesn't make any sense to me."

"Sir, I believe nothing but empty accusations are there."

The officer continued. "Betty's crossed the line innumerable times and should have had her ass fired years ago, yet you've allowed it to continue. You've allowed her to continue this behavior to the point that now we're having to get a bottle of what is likely excrement tested that she left on Pearl's front doorstep," the stranger shared.

Her boss winced. "I don't know anything about that, sir."

"No, you don't know anything about that, or at least you didn't until the interview today," he declared, authority in his tone. "Yet you also didn't explain how any of these were acceptable behavior. Meanwhile, this innocent woman has been attacked verbally on numerous occasions, even physically at times, has had her reputation impeached to the point that several other people have quit, citing the horrific abuse in the office for fear of retribution, and yet that one woman, this Betty, is still there."

By now, Grant was turning all kinds of red and purple, and the vein on his forehead was bulging like a fish out of water. "Sir—"

"Do you want to explain your preferential treatment of

Betty?"

"Sir?" Grant appeared to be at a loss for words.

"Especially now in front of the victim."

"Victim?" he asked, turning and glaring at Pearl.

At that, the commander, at least she thought he was a commander because of all the stars he wore, turned to face Grant. "Yes, right now, and in front of this victim who you have failed to protect."

Her boss immediately nodded. "I don't know anything about what Betty has done," he said, composing his face, "but Betty has always been a paragon of virtue, and she has always upheld the highest ideals of the office."

At that, Pearl's eyebrows shot up.

Jasper intervened, "Are you kidding? How could anybody possibly think that what Betty was doing was good for any office? The woman had been incredibly insulting and way the hell out of line."

The commander turned to look at Pearl. "You know more about this than any of us. What is your response to Grant's comment?"

"If Betty's treatment of me is what the lieutenant considers the *paragon of virtue*," she began smoothly, "then I'll say that Grant's judgment and standards of conduct are seriously impaired. I have been harassed. I have been hit. I have been defamed. I have been verbally abused on a regular basis by Betty, and you're right, several other people in the office have left because of it," she added calmly, knowing anger would not get her anywhere. "I had a purpose for staying this long. Otherwise I would have left myself."

"You should have left," Grant said, with a snarl.

"Lieutenant," snapped the commander.

Immediately the lieutenant shifted, not liking the reprimand, but obviously something was going on here. She then looked over at the commander.

He asked her casually, "Do you have any idea why the lieutenant has such a very different viewpoint on this?"

She shrugged. "He's never in the main office where Betty works. I don't think he's ever seen any of the abuse Betty handed out. I don't know that he's even attempted to address or to correct Betty's behavior."

"And yet it's his department?"

She nodded. "But he doesn't visit the department. He's never there. He's never seen Betty on the floor of the department. I don't think he has any idea of the hostile atmosphere Betty creates at work. Obviously the lieutenant knows who she is, and I can only assume he is sleeping with her." She winced, as she failed to catch the words, then forged ahead. The cat was out of the bag, and no backing away from that now. "That's the only explanation our workforce has come up with since anyone else would have been sent down the road by now. Honestly, I don't know why the lieutenant is partial to Betty," she added hurriedly. Raising an eyebrow, she turned to look over at Grant, who stared at her in shock.

"Hell no, I'm not sleeping with her. Who would ever think such a thing? And why would you say something so horrific? Do you know how much trouble you're in now?"

"You mean, I'm in trouble because I told you what the office gossip is? Yet Betty's not in trouble when she's called me a bitch, a whore, accused me of sleeping with my patients, sleeping with other staff members, not to mention leaving God-only-knows what on my doorstep? You let her get away with all kinds of nastiness. Yet, whenever I say something, I'm in the wrong?"

He nodded. "She had always been highly regarded in that department, and she's been there forever."

"Nobody likes her, much less *highly regards* her. And why she's been there *forever* is worrisome," she noted, slowly rising and glaring at him. "I know very well the stunts she's pulled and how unprofessional her behavior is. It reflects terribly on your department, but you don't seem to care. That's the real question. Why don't you care, Lieutenant?"

"I care about my department."

"If you do, sir, the question isn't why you have allowed her to remain there, but why it is that you don't give a crap how she treats your department or how she's ruined your reputation?"

"She hasn't touched my reputation at all," he snapped. "That appears to be all you're doing."

When she stared at him, then turned to Gideon, wordless, he took over.

"Meaning that Betty told you all about Pearl's behavior and the things she has said?"

"Of course," he snapped. "Pearl is horrible, and you don't know her like I do. She's been in my department just under a year since returning to base, so I know exactly what shit she's been up to."

"If that's the case," the commander said, "why haven't you dealt with Pearl?"

He sputtered, "Because I have people to handle it."

"And yet they didn't," Pearl stated. "Why is that? Why am I still employed? Oh, pardon me, I've just been fired. I forgot. But why is it I've just now been fired if I've supposedly been doing these things for almost a year?"

"I will not tolerate liars in my department," the lieutenant said. "You cannot tell me that Betty did any of these things."

She pulled out her phone. "I can probably show you then." She scrolled through to find an audio file where she had been recording patient notes at one point in time, when Betty had walked in, spewing her hatred in front of another team member.

When she found the recording, she looked at the lieutenant. "Maybe you would like to listen to this. It starts with me going through some of my chart notes." It played for a few minutes, then immediately Betty interrupted Pearl's dictation, and the things that Betty said made everybody's eyebrows shoot up.

Grant glared at her. "Betty wouldn't have said those things. You've doctored that recording."

She handed her phone over to Gideon. "Perhaps you can have your technicians double-check to confirm this recording hasn't been doctored by anyone," she suggested.

"Not only will our techs take a look at that," the commander began, interrupting them both, "but you, Lieutenant Hollick, are relieved of your duties pending a full investigation. That you even allowed this harassment in your department, allowed Betty to speak to one of your own staff members the way she has clearly been doing so blatantly is absolutely unbelievable."

The commander was gearing up for a full-scale bawling out, so she looked over at Gideon and nodded toward the door. She picked up her purse, turned, ready to walk to another room.

Immediately the lieutenant turned to her and snapped, "Oh no, you don't get to walk away from me right now."

"I wasn't walking away from you, sir," she clarified, with a smile. "I was affording you and the commander some privacy. It's quite obvious you're about to get a good old-fashioned ass-chewing, and I will spare you the indignity of having me here to witness it. But, hey, if you insist, I'll be sure to sit right here and take notes."

As he started to splutter in fury, the commander laughed. "I like her," he said to Gideon.

Meanwhile Gideon drew Pearl to him and held her close.

Then the commander snorted at Grant. "I do not like you, and I certainly don't like anything about what I've heard today. So, you better have a damn good reason why you have defended and sheltered a woman who has appallingly abused a coworker," he ordered, "and I want that today, right now, before you leave this room."

The commander was calm, and yet the authority that he exuded was unmistakable. "An investigation into this matter has already started, and it may well end up being one of these men who do it. So, if you have anything to do with the bottle of urine that your employee personally delivered to Pearl as yet another form of abuse, you better hope we don't find anything worse in that little jar."

"What are they talking about? They don't have any proof of that. She never would have done that."

Immediately Gideon turned and called their attention to the big screen in front of them and started to play the security video, documenting Betty's arrival at Pearl's house.

Seeing the video himself, the commander exploded, "Shit." He turned and looked at Lieutenant Hollick. "What do you have to say about that, Lieutenant?"

He just stared at the screen, as the commander continued to rip into him. "If you tell me it's been doctored as well, I will have every rank you've ever thought you had coming to you permanently wiped from your record," he declared. At that moment, two MPs came in, and the commander nodded to them. "Take him away."

"What do you mean, take me away?" the lieutenant sputtered. "I've done nothing criminal."

"You have," the commander stated, with a calm and calculated tone, his fury held just under the surface. "I don't yet know how far your involvement in this goes," he admitted, as he pointed around the room, then to the screen, "but something is very wrong in this picture, and I still don't understand your motivation."

Pearl looked over at her boss and saw a thin film of sweat on his forehead. He was also fisting his hands, as he tried to stand at attention. She gasped, realized what was happening here. "She's blackmailing you," she blurted out immediately.

Grant stiffened, as he turned and glared at her. "What? So now you're eavesdropping too?" he snarled, looking at her in fury, then turned away.

"No," she countered, "but, if you're not her lover, she's got something on you." She turned and looked at Gideon. "He's furious, but, more than furious, he's afraid," she explained. "Look at the way he's standing and the way he's clenching and unclenching his fists. But more than that, the cords on the back of his neck are struggling to release anger, but the anger is hidden, and guess why?" she asked, her gaze going from one of them to the other.

Jasper nodded. "We're never angry for the reason we think we are," he noted. "In this case you're right. I think it's fear. Look at the sweat."

"Right," she murmured, "and the only thing that makes sense is that Betty's blackmailing him."

At that moment, her boss broke down.

GIDEON LED PEARL to a small office area, which was a whole lot more comfortable. "The commander says you can stay in here. This is about to get interesting, but, unfortunately for you, it will have to be without your presence."

"I get it," she said. "I already feel bad enough for him."

He turned and frowned. "Seriously? For that asshole lieutenant?" So much disbelief and so much compassion were evident on her face that Gideon wanted to give her a hard shake. "I get that you're one of those lovely angels in the world," he murmured, "but this guy is compromised and has not done his job to protect his employees and needs to be held accountable for it."

"Maybe, but he is terrified, and, as somebody who understands that and realizes what she's done wrong in her life and how terrified she was that she would never get it back again, I can sympathize. So go on. Go deal with your problems. I'll sit and have a coffee." A small coffee machine was here, and she looked at it and wondered.

"Yes, you can have a cup," he muttered, then quickly disappeared. As soon as he was outside the room, he took a moment to think about what she'd revealed.

Jasper called out to him and asked, "What's wrong?"

Gideon shook his head and told him a little bit about what Pearl had just shared with him. Jasper stared behind Gideon at the closed door and smiled. "You better not let her get away from you a second time."

Gideon snorted at that. "I didn't plan on letting her get away the first time," he muttered.

"Obviously something was wrong."

"And I still don't quite know what that was about.

We've talked some, but we're not there yet."

"You'll get there," Jasper stated, with a smile. "She's got a hell of a perspective, not to mention an interesting view on life too."

"Particularly now that she's worried about this asshole. Understanding his fear, she's suddenly sympathetic to him."

"That makes her a good person."

"It does, but it can also make her a victim, and we don't want that."

"Speaking of which, did you ever get confirmation that the locks on your house were changed?"

"I don't know. I expect a confirmation call from Swede shortly."

"I still can't believe that he turned down another military job."

"I think he just wanted to go private."

"Maybe, but private after all those years?"

"Private allows him the freedom to work and the freedom to turn down jobs. Maybe that's why," Gideon suggested. "Swede's a good man. He's also been here a lot to help keep an eye on Mason."

"Mason would need to be sick for ten years in order to give everybody a chance to take a security watch," Jasper muttered.

"It's been a big help, and it does say a lot about the men."

"It does, indeed," Jasper replied. "I happen to love Mason. I told him when he married Tesla that he had one job and that was to keep her happy. He promised me that he always would, so, when he wakes up, I'll rib him pretty good because she's not happy now."

"What did Tesla think about Pearl's theory as to the motivation for our sniper?"

"She's giving it some thought, but she can't think of any instance where she was involved in a case and somebody lost everything that was important to them."

"But we don't know that, do we?" Gideon stared at him. "We almost never have follow-ups on our cases like that."

"True. We may have taken somebody out who was with the intended target. Somebody may have died in the crossfire. Somebody who we thought would recover may have ended up dying afterward," he suggested. "We'll have to go through each case to see who could possibly fit that scenario."

"That will take a lot of manpower, though Tesla could narrow it down with her software magic. However, she hasn't come up with anything so far."

"Then give her access to Mason's files," Gideon urged. "She can do it way faster than the rest of us anyway. You know that. She has the skill, and she alone can do what she does the best."

"That's true. I'll talk to the commander."

Gideon snorted at that. "Seriously?"

"She's got higher clearance than we do." Jasper nodded. "When I learned that, it was quite a shock to me, and not in a good way either."

Gideon laughed. "That's okay. If somebody on our side has clearance at that level and is as great as Tesla, she's good people all around."

With that, they walked back into the interrogation room, where both the commander and the lieutenant sat. The lieutenant looked a whole lot calmer now. He looked up, frowned, then turned away his gaze.

Gideon pointed out, "Pearl's not in here, and she won't

be coming in here."

The lieutenant's shoulders slumped, and he nodded.

"You've treated Pearl like shit in more ways than I can even possibly imagine," Gideon stated, "and, for that, it's not her you need to be worried about. It's me." The lieutenant stiffened, then turned and glared at Gideon, who just stared right back. "Don't ever doubt it. She's mine and always has been. And believe me when I say that I protect what is mine."

Grant stared at him, but the contest was already over before it began, and he nodded. "I didn't intend to hurt Pearl," he muttered, "but that Betty, she was poison right from the get-go."

"And in all this time you couldn't find a way to get rid of her? What about your ethics, Grant? What about manning up and confessing, ending the blackmail?"

He shook his head. "She kept giving me more and more reasons to, but, every time I tried, she threatened to expose every possible thing that she could find. She's got listening devices in my offices and even had them in my house somehow. Something is seriously wrong with her."

"What is it that she's got on you that you seem to think is so important that you kept it quiet?"

He didn't say anything.

At that, Jasper sighed and shook his head. "Seriously, you couldn't keep it in your pants?"

Grant glared at Jasper, and the commander groaned too. "Seriously?"

Grant shrugged and nodded. "It's a bit worse than that." His face flushed bright red as he glared at the other two men. "I would prefer that they don't know about it, sir."

"That's too damn bad," the commander barked. "You've

clearly been compromised, and I don't even know to what extent. However, these are two of my best investigators, and, if you think that anything you say will be held in confidence and away from them, you're wrong. That time has come and gone."

As the lieutenant stared down at his hands, it didn't take Jasper long to make the leap. "It wasn't a woman, was it?"

The commander sucked in a breath, and he asked in exasperation, "Grant, is that true? Out with it."

He lifted his gaze, and nothing but shame filled his expression as he nodded. "Yes," he admitted, his face completely red. "I realized I was homosexual through my young adult years," he began, and his words were forced out of him in a *whoosh*. "Honestly, I didn't understand very much about it. I fell in love with this young man, and we were together for a long time, until he broke it off. I ended up in Europe, where I met my wife and fell in love with her," he said, with a shrug. "I didn't quite understand that either, but it didn't matter to me. I fell in love with the person. Then one day he came back into town, and he wanted to meet up." Grant went silent.

"So, if you can move the story along ..." The commander gave an impatient wave of his hand.

After a deep breath Grant continued. "Yeah, so I was happy to see him. I was, but I didn't expect it to get out of control the way it did." He dropped his head in his hands. "We ended up in a hotel for the night."

"So, where did Betty come into this?"

"I have no idea how it happened, but immediately Betty had already heard about it and was blackmailing me, threatening me that my secret would lose me my wife, my job, everything," he said, holding back tears. "The more outrageous Betty got, the more I tried to push back, but she just pulled out more and more proof. I just couldn't do that, not to my wife or to myself," he whispered, as he looked away, his face flushed hot and red. "My wife will get hurt the most."

Gideon suggested, "Maybe it's time to just tell her the truth."

He raised his gaze and glared at Gideon. "What? You think that's just something I can tell her?"

"Yeah, do you think she didn't know about your previous partner? If your previous boyfriend came into town, it's like any other relationship," Gideon pointed out. "There must be trust. She trusted you, but you didn't trust her."

"Of course I trust her," Grant stated in astonishment, "I didn't even think I had to worry about trusting myself, but things got out of hand, and it just happened."

"You didn't trust her enough to tell her the truth, and that's a fact. You didn't tell her that you would see him. You didn't tell her what happened afterward," Gideon guessed. "That is proof that you don't trust your wife to have your back, which is sad. Now you'll face the consequences of whatever she wants to do about it now."

"I don't want to lose her," he said, staring at him, "I can't lose her to this. Plus, I have two sons. I don't want them to know."

"Why?" Jasper asked. "It might help them to understand who their father is, particularly if you're some hard-ass at home."

"Also," Gideon added, "when you're always fighting a certain part of yourself, I can imagine that conflict is constantly present—at home and at work."

"You're wrong," Grant argued, looking from one man to

the next. "That's hardly a conflict now, since I'm happily married, and I want to stay that way. I don't know what the hell that fling was about—old time's sake maybe. I just don't know."

"So, how did Betty know?"

"I think she heard me talking on the phone at work, setting up a meet with my friend. She must have followed us to the hotel afterward. We also walked around a park, though it was quite a distance from here. It was in the next county, not close to here at all. I certainly didn't expect to be followed, but she caught us in the park, as she has pictures. We weren't having sex, but it was enough," he muttered, with a wave of his hand, "and that was it. My life was over."

"Did you ever tell your boyfriend?"

"No, of course not," he said in horror. "That would make it ten times worse."

Gideon sat back and stared at him. "You don't trust anybody with your secrets, do you?"

"No." He gave a clipped nod. "I've learned the hard way that some secrets can never be revealed. People aren't ... Let's just say a lot of assholes are out there, and I couldn't afford to risk losing everything."

"And yet right now, here you are, in danger of losing everything," the commander declared. "How is it that you think you won't?"

"I was hoping you could find some leniency."

"You want leniency, even after you not only allowed yourself to be victimized and abused but worse, you turned around and allowed other people to be abused as well?" the commander asked, with a hard tone. "Where are the ethics and morals we stand for in that?" He looked over at the two investigators. "Gentlemen, if you'll excuse us, I need to have a much deeper talk with Grant."

Gideon and Jasper both stood up, and, as they walked to the door, the commander called back, "Gideon, do you trust me?"

He stiffened, then turned and looked at the commander and nodded. "Yes, sir."

"And yet I detect a distinct note of resignation in your tone."

"I trust that you will do whatever you think is best, sir," he stated, "but I'm acutely aware that doesn't mean it will be at all in alignment with what I see as a fit punishment."

The commander stared at him for a moment, and then, with a beaming smile, he nodded. "You are so right about that. However, hold on to that trust a little bit longer."

And, with that, the two men stepped out of the room. Gideon looked at Jasper and asked, "He'll let him off the hook, won't he?"

"Oh, I don't think he'll let him completely off the hook. I suspect he has something in mind, although we might never know. It could be about setting a trap for Betty because, if she's blackmailing him, it's a much bigger issue than Betty's ongoing harassment and delivering a bottle of urine to torment Pearl. Still, we need to know why Betty singled out Pearl."

Pearl interjected from behind them, her tone soft, "I think I may know why, but you'll think I'm crazy." When they turned, she shrugged. "I think it may have to do with you."

Gideon stared at her in shock, and she nodded. "She knew we dated before. She knew me, anyway, and knew about you, and she got infatuated with you."

"I don't even know her," Gideon said in astonishment.

"She had a picture of you in her purse. At least she used to. I don't think she necessarily knows anything about you," she explained. "She's built you up as being Prince Charming in her head, and, because she's never met you, it's easy to keep you there on a pedestal of perfection."

He snorted at that, and she smiled. "She knew that you and I were together back then, and that's why she hates me so much, and there is no going back from that level of revulsion. At least that's been my private theory. I had to come up with some reason for her having pictures of you, plus her harassment of me. It's as if, in her mind, I defiled something she considers perfect," she explained, with an eye roll. "Now that we are both in town again, that alone may explain the urine delivery at my doorstep."

Never in his wildest imagination could Gideon have ever thought this Betty conversation would turn back around to him. He stared at Pearl and shook his head repeatedly. "Are you serious?"

"Kind of." She nodded. "She had a picture, a picture of us."

"Us?" he asked, staring at her in shock.

She nodded. "I didn't have any way to tell you or to let you know at the time. This was awhile ago, but I told her that you were long gone and had left town. There were times when, out of nowhere, she would just look at me and laugh. Then it happened again yesterday.

"I didn't quite understand, but now I realize that maybe she knew you were here, and I didn't," she theorized, looking from one man to the other. "It never occurred to me that anybody would get so fixated on a person from afar, but she has been fixated on you, at least in the past."

"What picture?" he asked, still staring at her.

She smiled. "The one we took at the beach. Remember when we stopped and asked a stranger to take it for us?" she asked. "I was wearing a white T-shirt, and my hair was blowing behind me, and you had your arms wrapped around me. You are facing the camera straight-on, and my eyes were half closed against the wind. I never liked the picture that much, but you loved it."

"The picture we took on Coronado Beach?" he asked in shock. "Oh, crap."

She nodded. "What?"

"I used to carry that picture in my wallet."

She nodded. "I didn't know that you still carried it. I just figured you threw it away at some point, since we're not together anymore."

He stared at her in shock.

Jasper nudged him hard. "What are you thinking?"

"My wallet. I lost it at one point in time, and a woman called me and said she found it. I think I gave her a gift card and said thank you, and that was it."

Pearl tilted her head. "Have you ever met Betty?"

"No, I don't think so. I saw her in your home security video is all, but that was from a distance."

"Maybe you should take a look and see just who she is," Jasper suggested. "Maybe she is the person who returned your wallet."

"Was that photo still there, when you got your wallet back?" Pearl asked.

"No, it wasn't, and a few other things were missing as well," he said. "So I just assumed somebody had gone through it and then tossed it, before she found it. I was still happy to get it back but, no, that photo wasn't there." Gideon stared at her in shock.

Pearl murmured, "Betty's gotten a little bit weirder over the years, but she did seem to have this hang-up on you years ago."

"How long ago did you lose the wallet?" Jasper asked.

Gideon thought about it. "A few years ago, but not four or five. It was after we broke up, after you left."

"I wonder if she recognized me from the photo," Pearl said. "The way she just smirks at me every time she sees me is like she's got some secret."

"Maybe you're right, and the secret was that I was here in town again, and you didn't know yet. Because if Betty's the one who returned my wallet, and she's been stalking me over the last decade, whether in person or online, she would have known that I was somewhat local. She may have known each time I was back in town too. Getting my wallet back, I did spend a few minutes talking with her," he shared, "but not long, not overly friendly. Just small talk. I was there to pick up the wallet and to carry on," he explained, with a shake of his head. "People don't get obsessed over things like that."

"Whether it was an obsession with you," Pearl said apologetically, "or with hating me, I don't know. And who even knows if it made any difference in her mind. She didn't have anything to blackmail me with or for, like the lieutenant, but I think Betty's fixation with you, Gideon, became this delusional relationship in her mind."

Gideon looked over at Jasper, not understanding how any of this could have come about. "So, all her attacks against you," he asked, turning back to look at her, "are mostly because of me?"

She laughed. "That is a kind of justice, isn't it?"

Jasper held up his phone. "I just found this photo of her

off the website."

Gideon looked at it carefully and slowly nodded. "It could be her. It was a few years ago, and I certainly didn't take much notice," he muttered. He looked back at Pearl. "Did she ever mention me?"

"Oh, yes," she replied. "She told me what a fool I was for losing you, but now I deserved everything I got."

"But she didn't explain anything about what you did?"

"No, she sure didn't," Pearl noted cheerfully, "but then I had as little to do with her as possible. I was also wrapped up in my own reasons for coming back and a little confused as to how I felt about it and what the outcome might be," she shared, with a smile. "So I didn't spend very much time with her at all. Our jobs are very different, so we don't always cross paths. She isn't in the office all the time either, and, when she is, she causes me nothing but headaches. Thus I avoid her as much as possible."

"That's so weird," Gideon replied, as he shook his head in annoyance.

"I have made formal complaints and informal complaints, but nothing has helped, which is why I was looking at completely changing jobs again," Pearl admitted, "but it's not the easiest thing to do."

"No, of course not," Jasper agreed, "and, for shit like this, you shouldn't have to."

"Maybe, but after hearing how she's been torturing the lieutenant, I'm beginning to wonder if something is seriously wrong with her."

Gideon paced around the room. "People always say that mental illness is something to be watched for and how we should look out for it and help people. Betty is certainly irrational when it comes to her obsession with me and her harassment of Pearl. It would be easy to label her in layman's terms as mentally ill. Is that what we're saying?"

Pearl sighed. "I hadn't even thought of that obsession part of Betty for ages. She seemed so focused on making my life impossible, I just assumed it was all about her hating me," she said, as she looked over at Gideon. "You never had any other contact with her?"

He shook his head. "No, no way. I don't know anything about this woman, except that she returned my wallet."

"Any chance she's the one who stole it?"

He shrugged. "As soon as I say no, … we'll turn up something that means yes. Still, I don't have any reason to suspect her. She did give it back, minus the photo, but that now has me concerned. If she took that photo—and I don't know where else she would have gotten that photo except from my wallet—then that's where the obsession would have started, or gotten worse anyway," he suggested. "To think that she's been taking it out on you since you came back, that's just crazy."

"It certainly makes for a more interesting explanation," she noted, with a laugh, "and not exactly how I thought my days would be, when I decided to return." She looked around the room they were in and added, "Not that I expected to be here either."

"It's all good though," Gideon said comfortably. "It's a convoluted way to meet up again, so at least we're here."

They didn't say anything for a moment, both lost in their thoughts. Then she looked over at Jasper. "So, what's the plan? Will she get picked up?"

"She already has been, but no one has talked with her yet. I'm looking forward to it now," Jasper stated, with an odd smile.

"It would be nice to get that photo back if she's got it on her," Pearl noted. "It could be in her purse. The one time I saw it, she pulled it out of the lining, like a secret hiding spot." When the guys frowned at her, she shrugged. "One day she pulled it out, then looked at me and laughed, so I knew she recognized me from it. Absolutely nothing with this woman makes sense though," Pearl stated, shaking her head. "So keep that in mind. I don't want to say that she's not all there, but ..."

"But she's not all there," Gideon finished for her.

Pearl winced and nodded. "At this point, I would say that definitely something is amiss."

"Ya think?" Gideon quipped, as he looked over at Jasper. "I do want to talk to her."

"Yes, and so do I," Jasper said, "particularly now that we have another interesting angle here. We also have to remember where this is all coming from."

Gideon nodded. "Not only that but we must see if this is connected to Mason somehow. So far it doesn't appear to be, except these strangers were in both of our houses." He looked back over at Pearl. "I can't have you in the interview with Betty."

"That's fine with me," Pearl agreed. "I've had to deal with that woman enough already to last me a lifetime."

"Not anymore," Jasper promised.

She smiled and nodded. "You say that, but I haven't exactly had any support for the rest of the time I've been slogging through this mess on my own. So don't mind me if I withhold judgment on that."

Gideon nodded. "Don't worry. We'll get to the bottom of it pretty quickly now, and she may well be heading to jail instead of anywhere else. I need you to stay here for a bit, but

I'll be back," Gideon vowed, and she watched as he gave her a gentle smile. "You've done well so far."

She rolled her eyes. "That's like saying, *Just keep it up, and, with any luck, you won't screw everything else up.*"

He snorted. "Quit worrying about it. Just hold tight. We'll be back soon."

And, with that, Gideon and Jasper walked out.

CHAPTER 9

P EARL SAT IN the office and waited, played a game on her
phone, checked a few emails, talked to a couple friends,
caught up with the news. When she looked up again, hours
later, Gideon strode to her, frowning.

She asked, "How did that go?"

He shook his head. "She didn't show up."

"I thought Jasper told me that she'd been picked up?"

"She was, and then apparently they took her to her
house to get something, and she slipped right out from
under their noses. So she's on the run now," he shared, with
a concerned look. "I'm not exactly sure where she would go
or why, but I have a suspicion worth checking out. Do you
want to come?"

"Sure." Pearl hopped to her feet. "So, does it seem weird
that she was allowed out like that?"

"Not necessarily, since she was being picked up for questioning, not being charged, so maybe the officer
misunderstood."

"Maybe," she murmured. "Just her luck too. She also
spins tales, which makes everybody question why they doubt
her sometimes," she pointed out, with a small smile.

"The MP didn't have any reason for her *not* to go to her

house and get something. Then, while he was waiting for her, she ducked out the back."

"So now there's a real search for her, I suppose?"

"There is, but don't worry. We'll find her."

"You think you might know where she is?"

"I do. Come on. Let's go." With her racing alongside him, they got to his vehicle and hopped in. "You didn't talk to her much, did you?" Gideon asked Pearl.

"No, I can't stand the woman, didn't have anything to do with her, tried to schedule my shifts so that I didn't have to deal with her. It was hard enough just dealing with the gossip and the lies she spread about me, though it wasn't all the time. It was as if she would go on these fits and starts about it," she murmured. "Some days she was fine, and then other days it was just like parts exploding."

"That's a good way to look at it," he said, with a laugh, "not that anybody wants to deal with exploding parts."

"No, but, more often than not, we don't realize just what we're dealing with, except it's born of jealousy, rage, or something." As they drove along, she looked around and asked, "We're heading to the beach?"

"Yes, apparently she mentioned something about planning to be at the beach."

"Sure, but, if she had planned to be there, that doesn't mean she was still going there," Pearl replied. "That would make no sense, if you knew you had to go in and be questioned."

"Unless she didn't want to be questioned and went to the beach in order to fantasize about all she was doing."

"That just sounds off the rocker," Pearl muttered.

As they got closer, he pointed to a woman sitting off to the side on the rocks. "Would that be her?" he asked.

Pearl frowned. "It could be. I can't see her clearly enough from here."

"We'll get closer, don't worry." He parked, and they got out, then slowly walked in the direction of the woman.

When they got closer, Pearl sucked in her breath and nodded. "Oh my God, you're right. It is her."

"Good," he said, with a satisfied smile. He quickly sent off a text.

Pearl stared intently at Betty. "Surely we won't arrest her right now."

"You have a problem with that?"

She winced. "She already blames me for everything."

"Then it doesn't matter, does it? Look. Betty's made your life miserable, so I have absolutely no problem making hers a little miserable too."

"Oh, but she can't handle this," Pearl protested.

Moments later they stood before Betty.

Betty looked up and frowned. "Wow, look at that," she muttered in a strident tone. "When did you get back together? Did you seduce him again?"

Pearl winced at the loathing in Betty's tone. "I didn't know why you had been on my case since forever, but now I presume it has something to do with Gideon here. Yet whatever is between me and Gideon has nothing to do with you."

"He shouldn't be with you at all," Betty declared in a bitter tone.

"Who is it you think he should be with?" Pearl asked, suddenly fascinated and wondering just how far gone this woman was and if she was delusional enough to have created a relationship, even though she didn't know Gideon.

Betty sniffed. "He knows perfectly well."

Gideon stared at her. "I met you once, and I believe you stole a photo out of my wallet."

She stared at him in shock. "How dare you accuse me of stealing?" she cried out, as she got to her feet and turned to glare at him.

"The photo of me and him," Pearl pointed out, "the one that you flaunt to everybody else."

Betty paled and shook her head. "I don't know anything about it."

"Soon enough you'll be searched and your house as well," Gideon shared comfortably. "We don't particularly care whether you come back to the office with us right now or not. It is your full right to experience the whole *on the run* existence, if that's what you're going for," he murmured. "Or you can come in and talk to us."

"I'm not going anywhere with her," Betty spat.

"You have nothing to blackmail me with, unlike the lieutenant," Pearl noted. She stared at Betty, seeing something beyond what appeared to be a broken mind, and yet she looked so real on the outside.

"Blackmail?" Betty repeated. "God, I wish I had something I could blackmail you about, but you're such a Goody Two-Shoes. It seems you never do anything wrong. Do you know how sick I am of listening to the office defend you? Constantly telling me what a good person you are and that I should get along with you?" She snorted at that. "I have no intention of getting along with you. Some things are unforgivable."

"What did I do that was so unforgivable?"

Betty glared at her. "You know perfectly well."

Pearl tossed her head and smiled in Gideon's direction. "You mean, going out with Gideon, the man I love?"

Betty stiffened. "He would have to be completely out of his mind to choose you," she cried out. "Absolutely no reason why he would prefer you to me."

Gideon immediately stepped up and spoke. "I don't know you, but I have known Pearl for many, many years. She and I had a very good long-term relationship, but you? You are some stranger," he said, shaking his head. "I don't understand how you think you have a possibility of a relationship with me." He stared at Betty in amazement. "Did you just find the photo, see me, and decide that I am the one for you? You wanted something that wasn't available, so you created it? You wanted me, even if I didn't want you? Even if I didn't know you existed?"

Betty frowned at him. "Don't say mean things to me," she whispered, her bottom lip trembling. "You didn't even give me a chance. I'm way nicer than this bitch beside you," she said, snarling in Pearl's direction.

At that, Gideon shook his head. "I couldn't go out with anybody who treats other people like you did Pearl," he said. "That goes against everything in my world. So, if that's what you were thinking you could orchestrate, you're wrong. It can't happen."

"Of course it can," Betty declared, staring at him. "You just have to let her go."

"Let her go?" he asked. "It's that simple to you? Even if I did let her go, what good would that do?"

"You don't understand. We could be so good together, and I knew that once you met me, ... you would see that. You just had to meet me."

"Yet I did meet you," he said. "I don't want you."

"But you just met me for a second, so you don't really know me yet," she argued, with a crooked smile in his direction. "When I realized that you went out with *her*, I realized that she had ruined something for you because you're so perfect." Betty gave him a look of admiration. "I just knew that, if we could have the right moment together, you would see exactly how good we could be. The fact that you couldn't see that is all because of her. She ruined you for seeing how good life can be and how much I have to offer."

Gideon stared at Betty as if she were out of her mind.

"Just spend some time with me, and I'll show you how good it can be." When Gideon stared at her with a look that even Pearl didn't recognize, Betty shook her head. Turning to glare at Pearl, Betty shouted, "It's your fault, you sorry bitch! He would see it but for you. You ruined him, and now I'm left to fix it."

Just then several other vehicles arrived, and she looked back with a smug expression and sighed. "Oh, how sad," she muttered, turning to look at Pearl. "Finally my complaints are being listened to."

Pearl stared at her, then looked back to see Jasper walking toward them. "I don't think they're coming for me, Betty."

"Of course they are," Betty declared, with a wave of her hand.

"I don't think they look kindly on your blackmail and harassment," Pearl murmured.

"I didn't blackmail anybody," Betty declared, eyeing Pearl in shock. "Why would I? Everybody loves me."

"Everybody doesn't love you," Gideon said in a hard tone, "particularly Lieutenant Hollick."

She sniffed at that. "He's disgusting, and no way he should be allowed to have any authority. The things I could tell you about him—"

"We already know."

"I took care of that too," she shared. "I took care of his case, and it looks like I'll have to take care of even more." She raised both hands. "Why can't people just be decent, and then I wouldn't have to work so hard?"

Just then Jasper reached them, his gaze curious as he looked from one to the other. "Everybody having a nice friendly visit?"

"No," Betty snapped, pointing at Pearl. "Thank goodness you're finally here. You need to arrest her."

"Yeah? What for?" he asked curiously.

"She has ruined this man's life," she declared, throwing her arms out wide in an incredibly dramatic gesture, as she pointed at Gideon. "He has suffered terribly all these years. She's just ruined him."

"Is that why you went to her house and left the package on the porch?"

"Oh that." Betty gave a dismissive wave of her hand. "She just needed to know that's what she is."

"And what is that exactly?" Pearl asked.

"A piece of shit, nothing but human waste, get it?" she asked, with a triumphant smile. "You have ruined the last person you'll be allowed to ruin."

"I see, and what will you do about it?"

"I don't have to do anything now, since I've finally gotten the police to listen to me," she stated, with an eye roll. "It will be easy enough to deal with your being gone at work. It's not as if you do much of anything anyway."

"Of course not, after all, you're the one who does it all, right? You handle all the patients, write up all the reports, and somehow still find time to blackmail your boss."

"I didn't blackmail him because he's my boss," she

snapped. "He's a pathetic excuse of a man who doesn't deserve to live. The things he's been up to? ... It's just disgusting," she declared, with a dramatic shudder. "Do you know what he does? Somebody should have stopped him a long time ago."

"Somebody like you, I presume?" Jasper asked.

"If it takes somebody like me, then, yes, of course," she confirmed. "Somebody must make the sacrifice, after all. It's just too perverse to even think about." And then, with a brilliant smile at Jasper, she added, "So, go ahead and arrest her."

"No, I most certainly will not," he stated, giving Betty a harsh stare. "Pearl hasn't done anything wrong. But you, on the other hand, that's a whole different story."

She walked closer to him, then stopped at his words. "But that's not fair. She deserves to be put away."

"Does she?" Jasper asked. "I don't think so. I think that, in your own mind, you created a relationship with this man, despite the fact that he doesn't even know who you are."

"Yes, he does. Don't be ridiculous," Betty said. "I'm the one who returned his wallet."

"You returned his wallet and liked what you saw, so you created this relationship out of nothing," Jasper explained. "He doesn't even know you or anything about you."

"But he would, just as soon as he spent some time with me. He would fall head over heels. I just know it." Still protesting and explaining her point, Betty was led to a vehicle and placed inside. They could still hear her chattering away in the back seat.

Jasper returned to the two of them, shaking his head. "I'm not sure she's all there."

"She's not," Pearl agreed. "Looking back, I think it's

been a slow decline over the years."

Gideon smiled. "And you're still a nice person, even after all that?"

She shrugged. "Betty has hated me because she had a fixation with Gideon, the man I walked away from. I guess I shouldn't hold that against her. But the blackmail of the lieutenant? That's a whole different story. And his position against me? That's something I find hard to let go of," she shared.

"Not to worry," Jasper murmured. "All of this will come out in the wash."

"The lieutenant too?" she asked.

Jasper nodded. "No way to keep something like this private, not when it's gone this far."

She winced. "I feel sorry for him. I can understand why he was keeping it all quiet."

"Please don't protect him," Jasper stated firmly. "It's not your job, and he needs to face the music for his actions, just like everybody else in this mess." And, with that, he turned and walked away, getting into the vehicle and driving away, Betty still spouting off in the back seat.

Pearl turned to Gideon and repeated, "Human debris, *huh*, human refuse?"

"Yes, apparently that's what you are." Then he gave a brilliant laugh, wrapped her up in his arms, and said, "Now the good news is, we can mark her as not involved in the Mason case."

"And that just means"—Pearl frowned, as she tilted to look up at him—"somebody apart from Betty and her nonsense had another reason for breaking into my house. Plus, we had a different intruder in your house. Were the two intruders linked? Regardless, each one was playing some game."

"That's the problem. I can't believe that the decision to use your house was random. That intruder intended to squat there, I guess, and that just doesn't make any sense to me. Then somebody else already had the keys to my house—for however long, we don't know yet—and then trespassed on my personal property."

"We didn't ask where Betty found your wallet."

He nodded. "At one point in time, a jacket of mine was stolen, and my wallet and keys were in there. I have been using the spare keys ever since. I figured someone wanted a warm coat and wouldn't know which house the keys went to. However, now? ... Maybe that's where my particular intruder got my house key from."

"We need to go talk to Betty again," Pearl said, as she headed to Gideon's vehicle. "Because what if she and your intruder were working together? Someone found your jacket, and what are the odds that Betty got your wallet, while your intruder got your keys?"

"Yep." Gideon sighed. "I'll get Jasper to ask her."

"Where was your wallet found, according to Betty?"

"She supposedly found it on the sidewalk outside my home," he replied, "but I'm not sure. I'm not sure at all, as my jacket and keys never showed up. It's never that simple."

"No, and I'm not sure either. As for the keys, it is much more likely that it was a previous owner of your house or something else along those lines."

"And that could be too, except I replaced the locks when I moved in."

She frowned. "So, how about the guy who changed the locks?"

"Or somebody who worked for that company? Or, hell,

any person on base could pull that off."

"Right." She nodded. "These skills are way too easily found right here."

"They are," he murmured. "It could just simply be that some petty thief wandered into my house, but why? That's the question. Why? Normally low-level criminals don't intentionally enter a house that is occupied. They aren't interested in committing federal crimes. So they scout out their targets. If someone had been watching my house lately, they would already know that you were inside." He sighed.

"That's one of the hardest parts of the work that I do. You never know who's after you, or who might not like what you're investigating," he shared. "I thought it would be safe for you to stay with me, but now I'm wondering if I've put you in even more danger."

She snorted. "I don't know how you figure that, considering that both my place and yours have been crime scenes. Why don't we use one or the other and set a trap somehow, so maybe we can get to the bottom of some of this?"

He laughed. "That is a damn good idea. For now, let's head back home to my place, since the locks have been changed, and we have the security system ramped up. We can get some dinner and maybe have a quiet evening to ourselves."

"I'm all for that. It's been nothing but chaos ever since we ran into each other again. What about my house?" she asked, turning to him as they got into his vehicle. "When will I be allowed back over there?"

"I don't know, but I can ask. It's a different story there because, at my house, it was just an intruder, but at your house, … someone died."

GIDEON SET OUT dinner on the table, hoping that everything would stay quiet and calm, so they would have an evening to relax. Pearl was still with him, and, as far as he could tell, she was relaxed and comfortable in his presence and in his house. She was right about one thing. He had intentionally bought the house that they had often imagined and had talked about. It wasn't a particular house but a style of house, one they had set out together as being exactly what they wanted. He bought it soon after they had split up. He hadn't been prepared to let go of it, even years later when she remained gone. His reasons for wanting that house still remained, and he wouldn't give them up.

She smiled when she saw the spaghetti. "You always did make a mean spaghetti."

"I like to think so." He smiled as he sat down across from her, eyeing her and her plate. "Go ahead and eat up."

She nodded, picked up her fork and looked over at him. "What will you do now?"

"With any luck, we'll have a little bit of downtime this evening," he said, with a smirk, "before I get called out."

"Will you get called out?" she asked, staring at him in astonishment. "Don't you get time off?"

"No, not right now," he said, with a shrug. "Not with Mason still in the hospital and his case unsolved."

She winced at that. "I keep forgetting that's what started all this."

"I don't know that it started it all, but it's definitely the prime reason for me being added to the investigation team," he reminded her. "We just keep getting sidetracked with other problems—that may or may not turn out to be related."

"Right, who would have thought that Betty would have had anything to do with Mason being shot?"

"I'm not sure she does. It may just be that her drama happened to escalate at the wrong time."

Pearl nodded at that. "That does seem more probable in her case. When you think about it, how much of this nonsense can somebody stir up and get away with like Betty has?" she muttered. "It always amazes me, but blackmail does make complete and total sense. I still feel sorry for Grant."

"This wasn't something you did. Just remember that. You can feel all the empathy you want, but Grant still chose his actions and ultimately will be held accountable."

"I just don't want him to suffer too badly."

Gideon snorted, shaking his head.

She waved her hand. "No, I'm not naïve or innocent, or even a super nice person," she explained. "It's just that he's already suffered quite a bit. Now he'll suffer even more. Yet he knows what he did, and he'll have to face the music."

"In more ways than one. His wife was down at the office today, and I guess they had a difficult discussion."

"No matter how a partner looks at it, a fling is a fling. This situation would be all the harder since it was a past lover and one of the same sex," she noted.

"Yeah, that alone must be tough, if you're the wife."

"I certainly don't understand all of what's going on in their world, and it's not for us or for me to even get involved in it," she said, "but I can sympathize because he obviously hasn't truly made peace with himself."

Gideon nodded at that. "I won't argue with you on that one, but again, he was making his own decisions, right or wrong. He's also the one who opened himself up to blackmail and, worse, then allowed it to impact other people."

Pearl frowned. "Right. I can't help but wonder if Betty's done that with anybody else."

"I don't think so, but it's possible. The team is considering that angle as well. I think Grant's homosexuality was something completely against Betty's moral code. Whether she blackmailed Grant in the traditional sense or simply pressured him to secure her employment, I don't know."

"Right, I guess it's not blackmail if you're not getting money for it," Pearl noted in a dry tone.

"No, but she was certainly getting financial compensation in that she kept her job, when she was well past the point of doing her job," Gideon explained. "So it's still blackmail, just not for the cash payout we typically imagine."

"With a lot of people, the payout would have been much higher."

"Exactly. Still, the brass are not happy that Grant left himself open to *any* blackmail because somebody's always out there, willing to take advantage of our military's secrets. By doing what Grant did, and others finding out about it, he became an easy target. That is frowned on in the military, particularly within the higher ranks, because we can't risk having our high-ranking officers compromised in any way, either domestically or internationally."

"Yet none of us are perfect," she pointed out.

"Maybe that's why you're sympathetic to him," Gideon noted.

She winced and then shrugged. "You could be right about that. I hadn't looked at it from that point of view, and I'm not sure I want to either."

"You don't have to, and you don't need to feel anything other than detachment because it was Grant's life and his choices, not yours. And you were the injured party here. Remember that as well."

She smiled. "I have a hunch it's not always quite so easy for you to detach either."

"Lots of times it isn't," he admitted, "but not this time, because somebody else was getting hurt, ... namely you. I also find it much easier to let Grant take full responsibility because, while Betty was right in the middle of it, his own actions left him vulnerable. And he could have just owned his truth and all its consequences and stopped the blackmail from ever happening to begin with."

Pearl didn't say anything to that. When his phone rang a little later, she looked down at it and teased, "You almost got a full meal uninterrupted."

He sighed, picked up his phone, and said, "Hey, Jasper. What's up?"

"We got an ID on the man who broke into your house."

Immediately he straightened up and glanced at her. "Who is it then? How did you get an ID on him anyway? I thought we had nothing."

"We got his ID because he wound up in the morgue."

"Ah, hell no," he muttered, rubbing his forehead. "Somebody took him out?"

"Looks like it. He took one bullet to the center of the forehead."

"Crap, a professional hit, which means it was probably related to Mason somehow, though I don't understand why."

"No, I don't either. By the way, he's well known for breaking into houses, getting keys made, or whatever is needed in our world. Apparently that's his specialty, so he may not have had anything to do with you before."

"His specialty, *huh?*"

"Yeah, a nice distinction right there."

"That makes more sense to me," Gideon shared. "Though it still doesn't explain why I was targeted."

"It could just be because you're part of the Mason investigation. That could be reason enough," Jasper offered.

"Swede got my locks changed, and our dead intruder obviously got inside my house, but for what purpose? What is going on here? Why do you think they took him out?"

Pearl responded immediately, "Because he failed."

Jasper laughed. "I think she's right," he replied, still a hint of a smile in his tone. "It could very well be as simple as that."

"Yet did he fail? He got inside my house."

"He did, but Pearl was there. And I can't imagine a pro like your intruder did not already know Pearl was there. Plus, he headed for the stairs immediately, from what Pearl told me. My first guess would be that he was supposed to kidnap Pearl, as a way to control you, Gideon. Regardless of his true purpose for entering your home, your intruder was caught on your security cameras, and I suspect that's a good-enough reason for them to eliminate him."

"It's very much a permanent game they're playing, isn't it?" Gideon noted, turning to Pearl, who was moving the last bits of spaghetti around on her plate. Clearly she was finished, though he was unsure if it was due to the conversation or that she'd just had enough to eat.

Gideon got up, still talking to Jasper. "What do you need from me?"

"I've got Tesla digging more into your intruder, now that we have a name. Oh, and the coroner did note the guy had two legs of differing lengths, plus a surgical scar at his back, probably from a ruptured disk or something. That matches Pearl's remarks about your intruder suffering from injuries and possibly pain. Yet, so far, Tesla's not finding a whole lot more on your intruder. It's frustrating her, which I don't like because I don't want her upset, not when she's already got enough on her plate. The stress can't be good for the baby either."

"No, of course not," Gideon agreed, concern in his tone. "Do you want me to come down to the office? You can have Tesla hand off that deep dive to me."

"I'm already at the office, working on it right now," Jasper shared.

"I can head down there and help," Gideon offered, with a finality in his tone.

"For the moment, you're probably better off staying there, with Pearl, but I can send you some information to work on. We've also picked up your intruder's vehicle. It's probably wiped clean, but we will still take a good look."

"Oh, good. Send the file of what you've got so far. I'll start a review on that." And, with that, he ended the call.

"Are you leaving?" Pearl asked.

He turned, hearing something odd in her tone, then smiled. "No, Jasper will email me some stuff to work on here." He watched the relief take over her expression, and he nodded. "The intruder who broke into my house turned up in the morgue," he stated simply. "They have an ID for him, and they found the vehicle he was in as well."

"The morgue?" she winced. "What will you do?"

"I'll trace the vehicle, check the traffic cameras, and see if we can pick up any leads from that."

"Oh, good." She stared at him in amazement. "It sounds like things are starting to move."

"I would like to think so," he said, "but the thing is, every time another bad guy gets involved in this case, they are soon dead."

She winced. "It seems so deliberate."

"It is when the dead bodies are found pretty quickly. I don't know what the deal is yet, but I do know that any break we get right now is one we need to jump on fast because this has been going on for way too long."

"It hasn't helped that you've been sidetracked by things that didn't need to be a distraction. Betty, for instance."

He hesitated, yet shrugged. "I won't disagree, but I'm not at all upset with the way things have worked out."

She chuckled. "Is that a nice roundabout way of saying you're not unhappy that I'm here?"

"No, I'm definitely not unhappy about that," he declared, grinning at her. "But right now, I'll clean this up, and then I'll get to work."

"No," she said, standing up. "You cooked, so I'll clean up. It's only fair. You go get started in your office. I'll take care of this and will bring you a coffee in a bit." With that, she turned him around and pushed him from the room. "Go on. We have Mason at the hospital still, and we need to confirm he's safe before he wakes up. That way he knows he can recover without all that worry on him."

Gideon chuckled. "You'll get along well with Tesla."

"Maybe. I could use some new friends. It seems as if I've lost everybody over these last few years."

"That just means it's time to add some new people to your world," he declared. "We'll work on it once we get this case wrapped up." And, with that, he turned and headed into his office.

WHEN HIS PHONE rang, Pearl expected Gideon to be called out to some emergency. He took the call, but she never heard him leave. Frowning, she made him the promised coffee and took it to him. He was still on the phone and clearly agitated. When the call ended, he sighed, taking deep breaths.

"What happened?" Pearl asked.

"Sebastian was visiting his mom and dad—Mason and Tesla—at the hospital. He had stepped outside with a nurse to go get a cold drink, when a man dressed in a doctor's white lab coat tried to take him. Luckily the nurse was on the ball and didn't recognize the so-called doctor and yelled for an orderly. We also had two guards on our special patients, and one of them left his post to thwart the kidnapping. Still, our bad guy got away. But it's always better to save the victim, even if the perpetrator gets away. We'll get him later. I can promise you that."

"Oh my God. These people are evil."

"We'll double up the guards on Sebastian, no matter where he is, although he is staying with Tesla's dad for the time being. We will also keep him from visiting the hospital again. We can't have Mason's immediate family all in one room. It's too dangerous."

CHAPTER 10

P EARL CURLED UP in bed and stared out the window, wondering if she could sleep, what with the memory of her trip out the window and into the tree still very vivid. She knew she had an emergency exit now, and that was both a blessing and a curse because, if she could get out that way, it also meant that somebody else could get in the same way. That was something she didn't want to contemplate. Yet how could she not, knowing that route was available?

Finally she picked up her phone and texted Gideon. **Does this window lock?**

He answered immediately. **Of course.**

When a knock came on her door, she called out, "Come in."

He poked his head in and asked, "You can't sleep?"

"It's foolish, but, because I got out onto that ledge, I keep worrying that somebody else can come in."

He nodded. "Sorry, I should have shown you this earlier. I have a special lock on this window." He moved her to the window and pointed out the lock to her, showing her how it couldn't be opened from the outside.

She smiled as she looked at it. "Yeah, I would have been asleep hours ago if I had known that."

"My bad," he muttered, with the abashed tone of a little boy.

She burst out laughing. "It's all good. I'm happy to know it now." Climbing back into bed, she asked, "How's your work going?"

He shrugged. "Nothing to jump for joy about," he replied, with a crooked smile. "No leads so far, but I did track the intruder's getaway vehicle on the street cams—stolen of course—where he and the driver went a little farther from here to an outdoor parking lot. Then they stole another vehicle. I traced that vehicle, which sat in another outdoor parking lot. For about ninety minutes, a big rig truck was parked beside their vehicle, blocking the street cam. When that truck finally moved on, and we got a camera view back again, one person was in the getaway vehicle, but it's the dead man, our intruder. That's where he was found by a passerby, and, once he was moved to the morgue, our John Doe searches kicked in," he explained. "Of course the driver is unknown at this point and probably dead as well."

She sucked in her breath, then nodded. "They didn't leave much to chance, did they?"

"No, and I think luck has been on their side right from the beginning, like that semi truck," he shared. "Otherwise I could have seen a lot more of what happened, when he was killed."

"Did I hear you say something about a single bullet to the head?"

He nodded. "That's exactly what it was."

"So, execution style, as they say."

He nodded again. "In this case, tying up loose threads."

She winced. "*Nice.*"

"Yeah, not so nice," he agreed, with a smile in her direction. "When you think about it, this stuff shouldn't be happening, but it still does and not just here. I've seen it with guys like these pretty much everywhere."

"I'm sure you're right," she murmured. "Still, with all the things that can go wrong in your world, it doesn't usually involve this stuff, does it?"

"You would hope not. We don't want to be involved in things like this," he noted. "We would like to think something was peaceful and joyous about life. Yet, in the world I work in, we're always after people on the negative side of life."

"Do you find that it taints you?" she asked, staring at him. "Like your view of life? Or are you still able to put it away and see something different?"

"I thought I was putting it away, but I did have a period where I got a little bitter, a little less open to that more positive outlook," he admitted.

She winced. "That was because of me, wasn't it?"

He nodded. "Yeah, it probably was, but I moved past it eventually." He gave her a smile. "I reverted back to my usual personality," he said, with a laugh, "but not before a few people had pointed it out."

"Sorry," she murmured.

"Don't be. Sometimes you need to understand pain in order to truly understand joy." She sighed and he nodded. "Everybody is always talking about having a perfect life. ... When there's so much perfection and ease around, you can forget what other people go through at times. So seeing and feeling the bad side once in a while can make you a better person."

"It's made you a better person, for sure, but you already had a pretty good outlook, especially considering the work that you do."

He burst out laughing at that and then walked back to her bedroom door. "Now get some sleep."

"Will you be staying here all night, or are you leaving? Just tell me the truth. I can handle it," she said, narrowing her gaze. Then she took a moment and added, "But waking up and finding you're *not* here when I expect you to be, that will be much harder."

"I'm planning on staying, yes," he replied, "and I haven't heard anything different from my team. But remember that things like this can pivot on a dime. Sorry. I'm not used to worrying about other people being in the house."

"And you don't have to worry about me either," she stated firmly.

"Are you not nervous?" he asked.

"Betty, and two intruders, and escaping your house via the second floor aren't exactly the most wonderful events in my life," she said, "but I won't let all that ruin everything. I got away, and you caught your intruder, so it's a done deal."

"I didn't catch him," he pointed out.

"Fine, he got discarded. *Human refuse.* Wasn't that what Betty called me?"

He winced at that. "She's mentally sick. She needs some serious help."

"Still such a strange thing to consider. We all have our flaws and all that, but she was extreme."

"Are you sure you're okay? You've had some intense days."

She laughed. "Don't worry about it. I'm fine." As he stared at her, it was obvious that he was still worrying. She shook her head and waved at him. "Go on and get back to work. If you need to leave, just send me a text."

She waited until he walked out of the room and shut her door, then exhaled and relaxed because everything she had just told him was a pack of lies. How do you deal with an intruder one minute, then turn around the next and completely ignore it? It would take her a bit to get comfortable again, since both homes she'd recently spent time in had been compromised. She would get there. No way she wouldn't … because she had to.

Life would not dictate any more of these things in her world. She would do everything she could to maintain her independence and to not let something like this beat her.

The fact of the matter was, Gideon did have upgraded security here, and this was a topnotch house. So she appreciated everything he'd done to make it the home he'd always wanted. She would not ruin that for him, or for herself.

JUST AS GIDEON got settled in bed, hoping for a bit of quality sleep, Jasper phoned. "What's going on?" Gideon asked, yawning.

"Now an attempt was made on Mason's room tonight."

Gideon froze. "Seriously?"

"Yeah, so we've doubled up the guards once again. God knows we have enough volunteers to do that for years, without using any man twice. Dane was on shift at the time. He gave chase but didn't want to leave Tesla alone, just in case it was a setup. He gave us a bare description which wasn't terribly helpful, but we're viewing the hospital cameras now. This is just a heads-up that we're still under the gun and that everybody is figuring out what the hell they can do to help because, well, … it's Mason."

"No, I get it." Gideon stretched out on the bed. "So, what happened?"

"Somebody dressed up as a doctor came in to check up on Mason. Tesla was sleeping at the time, and Dane was standing outside, talking on the phone with the ER nurse about the upcoming schedule for Mason, when Dane noted that the doctor went straight into Mason's room. Dane didn't even hang up, as he raced inside to see the doctor casually preparing to inject something into Mason's IV line. He grabbed the doctor's hand, catching him by surprise. I am sending you the transcript of the report Dane made."

Gideon went straight to his computer, with Jasper still on the line, and opened the report. He skipped right to the statement made by Dane, since Gideon had gotten the basics from Jasper.

Doctor: I heard a guard had been posted, but I didn't realize it was this bad.

Dane: It is this bad, and you won't be administering anything to him.

Doctor: Why not?

Dane: His snooty tone triggered my suspicion of him. I immediately disliked him, distrusted him, and, while he was standing there, I called to a passing nurse. The nurse stepped in and asked, What's the problem? I pointed to the doctor. She took one look at him, shook her head, and asked, Who are you? He immediately muscled in, trying to get to Mason, and I blocked him. When he failed to get past me, he ran, tossing the nurse to the ground as he booked it. I gave chase but didn't want to leave Tesla and Mason alone, in case a second person was involved.

"Jeez, so they know where Mason is, and they know Tesla is there, and they don't care?"

"Exactly," Jasper replied.

"So now what?" Gideon rubbed his forehead. "We still don't have a reason why a sniper shot Mason, much less any workable suspects. We still don't have any idea who we're dealing with."

Jasper continued. "Exactly, and that's the bigger issue. We've got six of Mason's team sorting through files, some that they were players in, ones that others might have had something to do with. We hope to see if anything triggers memories as to a revenge killing of Mason. Right now, they've got about six cases currently flagged as possibles to be looked at, and we're doing deeper reviews on those now," Jasper explained. "But, as I'm sure you realize, Mason was involved in hundreds of cases."

"I'll grab some sleep, and then I'll take a look at those six, go deep into those myself. Do we have any idea why they were flagged?"

"Fatalities, fatalities of people with families, and one case where somebody was convicted, but he still maintains his innocence and blames Mason for the conviction."

"Why does he blame Mason?"

"Mason has notes in the file saying that the gunman was caught red-handed firing on women and children. It was considered open-and-shut."

"So why blame Mason?"

"Mason is the one who stopped him from completing what he considered his mission, which was to take out everybody in a specific family," Jasper shared. "And, because of that, he blames Mason and says that it's all Mason's fault, not his."

"*Great*, more psychopaths."

"When you do something like that, definitely mental instability is a factor."

"Speaking of which," Gideon added, with an odd tone, "Betty was seen by one of the psychologists here in town. Per the doctor's report, she's likely to be deemed unfit to participate in her defense, so unlikely to stand trial for anything she's done."

"*Wonderful,* so, in other words, Betty gets away with it all."

"Won't she be institutionalized instead? Regardless, if she gets away with it, I would agree with you. But honestly, I'm not sure she's *there* enough to even know that she's getting away with anything," he replied.

"I hear you," Jasper noted. "It's just frustrating. You want to see justice, but then, in Betty's case, you're not even sure what justice looks like. Apparently *you* became some image in her mind that she thought would be perfect for her. She did talk about you to this psychologist, saying that, as far as she was concerned, you guys were perfect together. She just needed to create an opportunity, the perfect opportunity so you could understand that."

"Even though I met her for five seconds just once?"

"Even though," Jasper murmured.

"*Great,* that just makes me not want to talk to people, … not even for five seconds."

"I get that too," Jasper agreed, with a note of humor in his tone. "More than that, if Betty is released, you need to keep that lady friend of yours safe. According to all the interviews done at her office, Pearl always held herself in very good stead. Her behavior was always exemplary, even in the face of Betty's harassment."

"That's Pearl, and I would expect nothing else. That's pretty much how she treats the whole world too."

"So, you won't let her get away this time, will you?"

"I didn't exactly let her get away last time," Gideon muttered in frustration. "However, once my trust is broken, that's a whole different story."

"Maybe, but, if you understand why she did it and what she was after, it should make it a little easier."

"Still doesn't make it perfect, though."

"So, does that mean you'll let her go?"

"I didn't say that," Gideon snapped in frustration.

Jasper burst out laughing. "I already know you won't let her go. I'm just wondering how long you'll make her pay for it."

"I'm not making her pay for anything," he protested.

"Oh, I think you are, … even if it's subconscious. She hurt you, and you would like very much for her to feel that pain."

"No," he argued. "That's not how I feel about her at all. That's not our relationship."

"No, it probably isn't, but subconsciously I'm not sure you're quite ready to let those past hurts go either." And, with that, Jasper disconnected.

CHAPTER 11

P EARL WOKE THE next morning, relaxed and calm. She remained in bed, wondering at the sense of well-being that she felt. She hadn't experienced that in a very long time. She was, indeed, still in Gideon's house, wondering how long she was supposed to stay before she got back into her own place. She didn't want to make any presumptions about the relationship they had slowly started to rebuild.

She got up, dressed, and headed to the kitchen to put on coffee, only to find Gideon already there, pouring two fresh cups. She stared at him and asked, "Did you get any sleep?"

He winced. "Do I look like I didn't?"

She nodded slowly. "Seems you had a bit of a rough night."

"Someone tried to attack Mason at the hospital." She stared at him in shock. "He didn't succeed. Our guy recognized that something was off and managed to thwart it. A nurse got knocked to the ground in the scuffle, but she's fine too, and we've doubled up on the guards, once again," he added, with a groan. "Not that we shouldn't have done that from the beginning, I guess, but we were minimizing our presence at the hospital. Now we'll have somebody both inside and outside."

"Sorry," she murmured. "I know you care about Mason."

"We worked together, and I respect the man. I don't want to see anybody in our group drop for something like this," he said.

"Are you going in then?"

"I am. What would you like to do today?"

She hesitated. "I'm not sure what I can do. Can I go back to my house? Go back to work?"

"I can certainly check and see. Forensics should be done with your place. I just don't know if they need time for anything else. As for you returning to work, I'm not sure about that."

She waited while he made the required phone calls. Then he turned, smiled at her, and said, "Your house is clear."

"Good."

"I need to warn you that it'll probably be a little on the rough side, with black fingerprint dust everywhere."

"Meaning that they made a mess, and I'm supposed to clean it up?"

He nodded. "Something like that."

"*Wonderful*," she muttered, under her breath.

"It's a problem, something that most people don't realize or expect. Anytime a major crime occurs, a forensics team comes through, and they don't clean up after themselves. That's for you to do. Plus, the original bloodstain remains as well."

"Wow," she murmured. "I know this armed stranger was shot in my house, but imagine if you lost somebody you cared for, and you still had to come back to that."

"Specialized companies do that kind of cleanup," he

shared, with a nod. "I just don't know how bad your place will be, now that forensics has been inside."

"I'll go look," she said, with a wave of her hand. "Besides, I want my wheels again."

He nodded. "How about I drop you off at the house then?"

And that's what they did. Of course he cleared the house to confirm it was safely unoccupied, then asked, "Are you okay to be here?"

"I am."

"Good. I'll call you in a little bit, okay?" Yet he stopped, hesitating for a moment, and added, "Please tell me that I don't need to be worried about you all alone here."

"I don't think so. Do we have any idea why my house was chosen in the first place?" He frowned at that and shook his head. "Go on," she said. "It's not likely anybody'll come in while I'm here. If they do, I'll let you know. ... Maybe I should get a security system. But it's a rental..."

Gideon nodded, as he looked around. "Yes but it's something we should look into."

"You can look into it later or I can just request a new residence." She shrugged. "It's not as if I have a whole lot of choice right now."

"Good enough," he replied, but he still hesitated.

"Gideon, I'll be fine. It's all right."

He frowned. "I know that in theory, but—"

She smiled. "I'm glad to see that you care enough to worry, but I'm sure I'll be okay."

"But I'm not," he murmured. "I don't feel good about this at all." Then he announced, "I'll just work from here today." She looked at him in surprise, and he shrugged. "I can't explain it. All I can tell you is that I don't feel good about leaving." She frowned and opened her mouth, but he interrupted, "No. Decision made. I'm not going anywhere."

She shook her head. "I should go to the office. I don't even know if I still have a job."

"You do, but you are off on sick leave at the moment, and they already have your patients covered."

"I still want to see it for myself. See if the harsh workplace element is gone. And I don't mean just Betty being gone. I want to see if all that meanness is gone."

Gideon nodded. "I understand."

She shooed him away. "Then go to work. I promise, if I go anywhere, I'll let you know. Plus, if anything weird happens, I'll let you know."

He shook his head. "No."

"Yes, go." When he glared at her, she laughed. "We can't both be stuck here. I promise I won't do anything stupid, and I will let you know if things turn ugly."

"But they turn ugly very quickly."

"Put a guard in here then," she suggested, raising her hands in mock surrender. "Get somebody you trust to stand guard, but you have to go. You need to deal with all these other issues."

He made a couple phone calls. "Okay, I've got somebody coming to stay with you, a friend of mine."

"Great, and what friend is this?"

"Tristan. He's one of the guys we were considering bringing onto the new investigative team."

She laughed. "Does anybody else know about this new investigative team?"

He grinned at her. "There have been problems with the old one for a very long time," he noted. "So we are just moving them out and bringing in an entire new team. So, you can bet we have vetted these people and have worked with them before."

It wasn't long before a knock came on the front door, and Gideon opened it with a smile. "There you are."

"It didn't take me long to get here," Tristan muttered. "I just had to wake up a minute first."

Hearing that, Pearl came up behind Gideon and smiled at the newcomer, "Hey, I'm sorry, but he's being extra paranoid."

"Given the circumstances, that's probably a good thing," the new guy said, as he stepped into the house. "My name is Tristan, by the way." He shook her hand and added, "And this old fart here has been a friend of mine for a very long time."

"We've been friends a long time too," she said. "Funny how I've never met you though."

He smiled at her. "Oh, but I've heard about you."

Instantly she frowned. "In that case, maybe you aren't here so willingly."

He burst out laughing. "Whatever is between the two of you is between the two of you. Although maybe I'll just coerce you away from him."

She rolled her eyes at that. "Nothing to coerce me away from. What we had was a long time ago." Ignoring the look Gideon sent her, she added, "Besides, I have to check out my workplace today. I can't just sit here and do nothing for the rest of my life."

"Understood." Tristan smiled. "So now the question is whether you want me to come with you to your office or sit outside and stand on watch."

She groaned. "Seriously, you don't need to do that either."

"Hey, you mentioned a guard, and I made that happen," Gideon pointed out, "so no arguing. If he says jump, you jump. If he says you lie down, you lie down."

She stared at him and asked, "Seriously?"

"Yes, ... seriously. I trust Tristan with my life," he explained, eyeing her intently, "and, in this case, I trust him with your life too." Gideon turned to glare at Tristan, who was grinning as bright as the sunshine. "And regardless of what she says, definitely something is between us, and I'm doing everything I can to get us back on a normal footing," he muttered, as he walked out the door. Then he stopped, turned around, and walked back to her. After he gave her a hard and long kiss, he muttered, "And don't you forget it." With that, he was gone.

Tristan burst out laughing at the look on her face. "Don't tell me that you didn't know," he said, breaking the silence. He sniffed the air and then noted, as if nothing had happened, "Coffee. I could use coffee." As she led the way to the kitchen, he continued. "Seriously, you can't still be confused about Gideon."

"We haven't talked about it," she said, uncomfortable with the conversation. "I wasn't sure he was at all interested in going back to what we had."

"Oh, I don't think he is. I don't think he's interested in that at all," Tristan clarified. "But I don't think that's the same thing as figuring out if you have something better to move forward to."

She stared at him for a long moment, and then smiled brilliantly at him. "I like the sound of that. It sounds a whole lot better than what we had."

"Somewhere along the line he might need a little more explanation of why you walked."

"I don't have one," she admitted, with a sour expression, "and that's probably something that'll hold him back."

"No, it won't," Tristan argued, with a smile, "so don't go putting thoughts and words in his mouth. He's very capable of making his own decisions and very capable of sorting out what he needs to sort out. So just give him some time and space, and he'll get there. Like he said, as far as he's concerned, you already have something between you. Now, do you have any food here?"

She watched in amazement as Tristan rummaged around in the fridge, pulling out eggs, then checking the freezer, pulled out some sausage, and asked, "Did you eat?"

She nodded. "I had toast."

He winced. "Toast? How is anybody expected to do all this work on toast?" He asked, "So if I make sausage and eggs, will you have some?"

"Sure," she said, surprised and yet amused to see him completely at ease as he took over her kitchen. "I guess you don't worry about being at other people's places, do you?"

"No, I sure don't." He gave her a big grin. "You can spend an awful lot of time worrying about crap like that. Whenever you can, get into the groove of what life currently gives you and just enjoy it."

And next followed one of the strangest lunches that she'd ever experienced, and yet it was fun. It was filled with laughter, and somehow the time went by so quickly that she was flummoxed when she looked down at her watch and realized what time it was. "I don't know if that was done on purpose on your part," she noted, "but you've been here for hours already."

"Hey, what do you mean, *on my part?* It's easy to spend time with me. I work hard at being a nice guy. Plus, I'm supposed to be here, by your side."

She laughed. "I didn't mean it that way. I just meant that somehow the time disappeared so quickly, and I wasn't expecting it."

"That's because you're spending way too much time worrying and fussing, when you should be just relaxing."

"Maybe I'm still adjusting. After the big fiasco we had at my place, I ended up staying at Gideon's. Then we had somebody break in there," she told him. "I ended up climbing out the second-floor window and up a damn tree to get away from the intruder in my PJs. Afterward, I had to somehow make it back inside again, all while not on the ground. So, getting some sleep there last night was hard to manage, but I finally did it."

"Oh, it all sounds exciting," Tristan replied, his face lighting up with interest. "Tell me more."

She rolled her eyes. "Are you for real?"

"Of course I'm for real," he declared, with mock innocence. "You just don't know what you're missing."

"You could be right." She sighed. "With somebody like you, I would never be sure who and what you are."

"I'm just a guy, somebody you can trust, somebody you don't have to worry about, no pressure. I'm just here. And"—he let the word hang there for a moment—"I won't make you do something you don't want to do."

"Does that mean I can go to my office, all on my own?"

"Ah, no, no way," he stated, with a big grin. "I plan to stick to you like a second skin."

She rolled her eyes at that. "I would much rather have Gideon."

He burst out laughing. "Now that is something you could have mentioned earlier. I was starting to wonder if you even cared about the guy."

She gave a shy smile. "I've never cared about anybody the way I care about him. ... Don't ever think otherwise."

"As long as you understand the reasons why you did what you did that broke the man's heart," Tristan replied, "I'll let it be."

"No, I don't understand," she said, "but I'm trying to."

"Just don't ever do it again," he added, a hint of a warning there. "Most of us will allow a mistake once, but a second time, we're put on that same nightmare path of pain, we can't do it. Once is more than enough."

"I didn't intend to hurt him. I was just running from everything."

"You succeeded, but, in succeeding, you also caused him a lot of pain."

"I know," she murmured. "I don't want to do that again."

As it was, when she got to work, everybody was excited to see her. She was surprised at the greetings but heartwarmed by the seemingly enthusiastic and honest responses when they all realized things were changing and that Pearl would still stay with them, at least for a while. After a few minutes, everybody slowly meandered back to work, and things started to settle in. Her boss walked over and asked, "How are you doing?"

"I'm okay. It's been a rough couple days."

"I'll say," Maria muttered. "It's been a little crazy here too, what with all the investigators and whatnot."

"I'm sorry you had to go through all that."

"Did Betty deliver something to your door?" When Pearl nodded and told her what it was, Maria paled. "My God, she's lost it, hasn't she?"

"I think that's the assumption right now. I don't know what'll happen next."

"Right." Maria stared in the direction where the main offices were. "I'm not sure what'll happen either, but it's not your fault, so don't you worry."

Pearl chuckled. "It would be nice to think that whatever happens next didn't require any involvement from us, but I'm not so sure we'll be that lucky."

"You're being awfully forgiving, considering what Betty put you through."

"She's not here now, and she won't be back," Pearl noted. "So I'm just glad the problem has resolved itself." And, with that, she headed to her desk to have a look at her schedule and to gather her things.

When Diane walked in a few minutes later, she hugged Pearl. "I've taken over some of your patients for the last couple days. Do you know when you're coming back full-time?"

"I would like to say tomorrow, but that may be a little early yet."

Tristan looked over at the physical therapist and shook his head. "Pearl won't be back for another couple days at least, and even that is just my best guess." Pearl stared at him, and he nodded. "We have more shit to get fixed first," he stated, without any reservation.

Pearl winced and nodded. "There you go," she told Diane.

"Okay, in that case, do you have a few minutes to go over some of your cases?"

"Sure."

And, for the next hour, she went over several of her patients, going over some of the treatments she had programmed and set up, all ready to go. When they were done, and Diane disappeared, Pearl looked over at Tristan and just exhaled. "Seriously? It'll be that long?"

"Yes, seriously. Remember how a gunman broke into your house?"

She stared at him. "I was trying to forget that, until you brought it up again."

His grin flashed. "So, isn't it a good thing that I brought it up then? All kidding aside, it's not something we can afford to forget."

"Maybe not *forget*, but I was hoping there might be a solution that would allow me to get my life back to normal. It's pretty hard to even figure out how these two events are connected."

"Oh, I agree with you there," Tristan confirmed, with a flat look in her direction. "I'm new to Mason's investigation and to your mess, but I've been working in the background. If you want my preliminary take? Some of this isn't making a whole lot of sense."

"Exactly. So why my house?" she asked. "And why Gideon's?"

"His house because he's an investigator, and obviously somebody tagged him, saw him, and considered him to be an issue. I would say it's Mason-related. And your house, I initially suspected ... was because of Gideon. Now apparently it wasn't so much about you and him and more about that location."

She shook her head. "Yet we've only just reconnected."

"Yes, but that doesn't mean your history isn't on the internet."

She paled at that, and then she nodded. "There's probably quite a bit of us out there in the world wide web because that's life these days, isn't it?" she said bitterly. "Once anything is on the net, it seems to stay there."

"Even if it doesn't stay there, people who have any decent computer skills can still find it," Tristan pointed out. "So, when you first saw Gideon again, was anybody around?"

"Sure. We were in the hospital—no, actually in a stairwell," she clarified, with a nod. "We didn't hug or anything, just acted like old friends, catching up. Then we went different ways. I went downstairs, and he continued on. So, even in the stairwell, people could have seen our interaction, but I don't know that anybody else was there or was paying attention. Honestly, I was so shocked at seeing him, I wasn't aware of anyone who may have been around."

"Which is probably the same for him."

"Ask Jasper then," she muttered, with a wry look, "because he was there at our initial meeting too."

"Interesting. Maybe I'll do that. At least see if he recalls anybody seeing you together."

"I may have called a friend from my office and told her that I saw Gideon. Maybe someone overheard that conversation."

"Okay, then who did you call when you discovered somebody was in your house?"

"Him," she said, without thinking about it.

"Did anyone see that happen?"

She stared at him and frowned. "I don't know. Gideon arrived pretty quickly. I had such a bad feeling that I didn't even go inside. Then, while waiting in my car, I saw Betty drop something off. I was already rattled, but nothing prepared me to see someone open my door and grab the package off the porch. Knowing Gideon was in town, I didn't even think twice about who I should call," she explained.

Tristan seemed to be completely okay with it and just brushed aside her explanations. "That's not the main issue. The main issue is whether anybody saw Gideon, whether with you initially, in the stairwell, or when he showed up at your house."

"Oh, right," she said. "Some stranger was on foot in the neighborhood. When I didn't see any parked car on the street, I got nervous about that too."

Tristan nodded. "The team is scouring the street cams and any doorbell cams to see if we can ID him. But then you moved to Gideon's house, right?"

"Yes, that's correct."

"And the bad guys brought in somebody well known for getting into houses," Tristan shared, "so he was obviously somebody they had at the ready."

"But why kill him, if he was so skilled then? I assumed it was because he failed."

"And that could be, but I'm not sure that it was *just* because he failed, as much as they didn't want him around to talk about his involvement."

"But they might need him again," she protested. "Why would they get rid of skilled labor?"

He smiled. "We're not sure that these particular Mason-related bad guys killed him. It could have been an attempted car-jacking or something unrelated, but who knows? Maybe the lockpick said something. We don't know what happened, but he was killed very soon after leaving Gideon's house."

She grimaced. Both intruders died. Hers at her own place. She was saddened at the thought that somebody had broken into Gideon's house and then had died so quickly afterward, just because he'd done the job he was hired for. "So, you're saying, someone saw me with Gideon, and that set off these two intruders and whatever else?"

"You certainly could have been tracked, and they would have noted Gideon right from the beginning when he came to your house. They would have had his name and background immediately. Once that was done, it would have been a case of checking to see what you did afterward. Of course Gideon was also responsible for their man's death at your place."

"Right," she whispered, "and that was a little upsetting too."

"Sure it was, but Gideon was defending himself, and nobody'll argue with that."

"No, I don't imagine so." She took a deep breath. "Still, it doesn't explain, *Why me? Why my house?*"

"I don't think it was about you, as much as your place."

"Yeah, everybody keeps saying that," she replied in frustration, "but we don't have any explanations as to who and why."

"No, but the property across from you is an interesting one."

She frowned. "It is? Interesting in what way?"

"Your place is the only one with a view of that home across the street."

She nodded slowly. "That's true. I hadn't considered that."

"So, if anybody wanted to keep an eye on anything going on across the road, then your place would make a whole lot of sense."

"Okay, so they invaded my place so they could spy on whatever was going on across the road. But do we know who lives there and what is happening over there?"

He hesitated, then nodded and relented with a huff. "I've already been there and done that research. It was occupied by somebody in the military, and he committed suicide."

She stared at him. "So, why watch a dead man's house?" she asked.

"I guess maybe they wanted to know if anyone showed up there."

"Or," she guessed, staring at him intently, "maybe he didn't commit suicide at all?"

AT THE NAVY'S Investigation Department, Gideon took over an empty office. He was busily catching up on recent reports, reading the six possible revenge cases, figuring out his schedule, and determining where to go next. He was distracted by all these thoughts when his phone rang. ID'd as Tristan, Gideon answered, only half focused on the call. "Everything okay?"

"Yes, everything is all right here. However, your girl-friend has an interesting suggestion."

Now fully at attention, he frowned and asked, "What did she say?" Then he listened as Tristan explained about the suicide across the road.

"We didn't consider that, did we?"

"No, we read the material presented to us and accepted the suicide finding at face value," Tristan replied. "I give her credit that she's not quite so gullible as some might assume."

"No, she isn't," Gideon agreed, a smile in his tone. "Jasper and I have commented many times these last couple days on the different ways her mind works. This is another great example."

"I like it," Tristan said, with a laugh. "I'm not sure what we're doing next. At the moment, she's going over treatment plans and exchanging notes with another therapist, and then we're leaving. I've told her that she's not likely coming back to work for a few more days. I think we need to check into that suicide."

"You're right. I'll switch to that immediately," Gideon replied. "I've had my fill of reading reports. On my way home I'll take a look at the dead guy's place across the way from Pearl's."

"Are you sure you want to do that?" Tristan asked.

Gideon frowned. "Any reason not to?"

Tristan hesitated. "Obviously you've already been identified in this. So butting your nose in again might just trigger something."

"Good," he snapped. "I sure as hell hope it does."

"What about *her* though?" Tristan asked. "You're putting her right in the center of it."

"Damn it," he muttered.

"How about you come straight to her place, and then I'll take a run past the dead guy's house."

"*Great*," he muttered. "That's the problem with most of us right now. We're spread a little too thin, and we can't take any chances."

"No, we can't take any chances, and you wouldn't want to. The stakes are too high, and we have too much chance for things to get ugly in a permanent way."

"Yeah." Gideon sighed. "I'll do some related research and share any information I uncover. Then, if you want to check it out afterward, that would be great."

"Sounds like a plan. Sorry to interrupt your report reading. Just giving you that heads-up. I think it's a good idea on her part."

"Agreed, and not exactly something I considered, which pisses me off because we don't often walk away from a suicide without really checking that it was a suicide. However, somebody may still be looking for our suicide guy, since he was under investigation."

"For what?" Tristan asked.

"Theft from the base. And the investigation file? ... It's a little on the skimpy side."

"And yet if it *was* an investigation ..." Tristan began, leaving a hint hanging there.

"Exactly, the file should be complete."

"After the navy's own investigative team abandoned Nicholas, their own team member, we now have one more thing to talk to the rest of the original investigation team about." Tristan gave a hard laugh. "I'm starting to see why you might need to replace everybody." And, with that, Tristan ended the call.

Gideon got up and walked into the main room, where Jasper was talking to Morgan.

Morgan looked up, then frowned in exasperation. "Now what? It seems like every time you guys come in here, you find more shit."

"Yeah, sure seems like it," Gideon agreed. "What's the deal with this Drew Honeycutt?"

"Drew Honeycutt?" Morgan frowned.

"Yeah, apparently he committed suicide. Yet he was being investigated for theft on the base."

Morgan nodded. "Right, now I remember. He killed himself just after we brought him in for questioning. We felt

DALE MAYER

shitty there for a while because ... honestly, we put a little pressure on him, and it appeared he went home and blew his brains out."

"Blew out his brains or blew up his face?"

"Same thing. What does that matter?" Morgan asked, with a shrug.

At Morgan's comment, Jasper looked over at Gideon. "What are you thinking?"

"I took a look into that case, and the file is pretty empty."

"That's because it's closed," Morgan noted. "You have to go into the different areas in the database." He quickly showed him where the closed files were. Then he looked at the two men and added, "I'll head home for the evening, if you guys have nothing else to go on for now."

"No, we don't," Jasper said.

They exchanged goodbyes, then Jasper walked over and asked Gideon, "What's going on?"

"Are we alone?" he whispered.

"We are, why?"

He quickly told him Pearl's theory as relayed by Tristan. Jasper stared at Gideon for a long moment. "So, does she want a job in our department?"

Gideon laughed. "It wasn't something that came to me immediately when we were looking at this, and I should have considered that."

"Why though? Why would any of us consider it? We trusted the navy's investigation file, as is, which, under normal circumstances, is trustworthy," Jasper noted in frustration. "And that's part of the problem. The Mason case and these related ones have had us flummoxed from the start."

"Not so much that we're flummoxed as we're affected. Me because of Pearl and her sudden arrival into my world, but also because it's Mason," he declared. "We're all off a bit because it has to do with him. We want to solve this, and fast, but instead, I feel like we're missing potential avenues of investigation."

"Seems like it. Apparently it's a good thing we have Pearl around," Jasper shared, with a half laugh, "because she keeps coming up with shit I hadn't considered or just accepted at face value, and you're right. It's pissing me off."

"Right," Gideon agreed, with a wry look. "She's right, and we don't know for sure whether Honeycutt was a suicide or not. But did you hear Morgan's response to the question about him blowing off his head?"

"To him, it didn't matter because one is the other, isn't it?"

"So, let's make a phone call to the morgue and see if they have anything on that."

It took a bit to get through to the doctor in question, and he was cranky when he answered the phone. But when he realized what the question was about, he immediately became quite interested. "It was a facial headshot, but he had an ID on him. Plus, he was under investigation, so it's quite possible his identity was falsified. I hate to even say that right now because it'll just piss me right off. Still, I had an ID from someone else. So I'll have to go into the office right now and check this out."

"Do you have any idea what happened to the body?"

"Yeah, it was cremated."

"Shit."

"Yeah, but wait. As is my personal habit because we're hoping to create better databases in the future, I did take a

DNA sample."

"Well, now that is damn lucky."

"No luck about it," the coroner declared, still rattled that he may have missed something. "Remember how that's my own personal habit, and I cultivated it. So luck doesn't begin to enter into it. On the other hand, if I had realized something was not quite right about the case, I probably would have done other things differently too, and that's just pissing me off too."

"We don't know for sure that we have a case of mistaken identity or that we have somebody who didn't commit suicide. No point in speculating yet. But when you say you took a DNA sample, did you find anything else?"

"I took multiple samples from him. He had a history of a certain cancer in the family. So I wanted to do reports on it, and I needed blood for testing. However, this is now old blood, and I kept it for *just in case*," he explained. "Do you know if any family exists, someone we could test it against?"

"We shouldn't even have to," Gideon said. "His DNA should already be in the military database. It's not as if he was anonymous or something. Honeycutt was a captain, after all."

"That's quite true. Okay, I'm heading into the office. I'll let you know what I find."

He ended the call, then turned and looked at Jasper. "What do you think?"

"If Honeycutt was stealing from the base, and these guys are keeping an eye on the house, what it's all for?"

"Maybe by committing suicide, Honeycutt was getting out of something he may have owed them for, or maybe he had something planned."

"It's the *something planned* that gets me," Jasper muttered, with a hint of exasperation. "It's been too long since the sniper shot Mason, and we are still getting nowhere in the investigation."

Gideon nodded. "Because we're still looking for a ghost, someone responsible for Mason's sniper shot. What did this Honeycutt guy do?"

As they looked it up, they both whistled and nodded.

"Now *that*," Gideon noted, with a wolfish grin, "makes it even more interesting. Honeycutt was a sniper on active duty. Plus, *uh-oh*, look at that. ... Look at his history. A little bit more is here, although not a whole lot. Looks like some suspicions were raised about his smuggling weapons."

"What the hell do you mean, *suspicions?*"

"Nobody did an investigation."

"Nobody did anything?" Jasper asked.

"Because he killed himself and left a note, it looks to be all tidied up quite nicely." Gideon looked over at Jasper and asked, "Is it just me, or does this department seem to tidy up things a little too nicely?"

"Yeah, but, before you start digging into even more of the original investigation team's files, we've got to focus on those that deal with Mason's case first."

Gideon nodded. "When we have wrapped up Mason's case, we'll take a long deep dive into how this department operates—or doesn't."

Jasper sighed. "I've had a couple talks with the brass upstairs, and, of course, they want me to come in, but I'm not sure I'm quite ready for such a fight."

"It won't be a fight at all. You'll come in, clean house, and walk out, and everybody will be wondering what the hell just happened."

Jasper laughed. "I won't argue with that." He smiled.

"Yet we've got to deal with this first. By the way, Masters is out there somewhere. We need to connect and see what he's found, if anything."

"Of course," Gideon agreed. "I haven't seen any sign of him since I've been back."

"No, but that's because I've got him off looking into all kinds of stuff. He's been running his way through everything that's happened recently in Mason's life, heading up that part of our investigation. He's also dealing with Tesla as much as he can, to see if there's anything active we can investigate."

Just then the door opened, and Masters walked in, glaring at them and grumbling at Jasper, as he reached out to shake Gideon's hand. "What shit job did you give me now?"

Jasper grinned at him. "This shit job you'll absolutely love."

Masters brightened. "Yes, please, give me something else. So far, Tesla won't let me get anywhere close to any of the cases that she's singled out. She says she won't ruin anybody else's life until she's damn sure."

"I have another name for her to look at," Jasper shared, holding up Drew Honeycutt's file.

"What's this?"

"Some navy captain who supposedly committed suicide after finding out he was being investigated for theft on the base, possibly involved in arms smuggling," Jasper shared, as Masters's eyebrows shot up. "Won't matter if we drag his name through the mud, even if something is there. As things currently stand, he shot himself in the face. However, we just talked to the medical examiner, who didn't question the ID found on the body or the in-person identification also provided to him. The coroner ruled it a suicide, and that was that. The body was cremated. But the coroner kept a DNA sample. He's running it against the database."

"So then what? Now you're thinking the suicide guy had something to do with this?"

"We don't know for sure," Gideon admitted, "but the place where he lived is directly across from Pearl's, which is where we had the first break-in, with a gunman who pretty-much acknowledged his illegal presence in her home had nothing to do with her, but it was all about the location of the house."

"Right." Masters frowned, as he asked them, "Did this supposed dead guy have any decent field experience?"

"Yep. Not only that, he was a sniper," Jasper shared, with a hard grin.

At that, Masters gave Jasper a high five. "Bingo," Masters said softly. "Now we're finally getting somewhere."

CHAPTER 12

AFTER CLEANING UP the majority of the black fingerprint dust from most of the first floor, Pearl sat in her
living room chair and stared out at the house across the road.
She was inside her own place, the men standing around,
talking over her. The bloody mess remained to be cleaned
up, but she just disconnected from it the moment she'd
walked in earlier this morning. She wasn't even sure what it
would take to get her to acknowledge the blood on the floor
and to do something about it. It was just beyond her for the
moment.

Gideon sat down on the chair beside her. She didn't
look at him, didn't look at anything. "What are you thinking?" he asked.

She pointed at the house across the way. "I was thinking
about how little we know about others in our world," she
murmured, "how little we interact with anybody. Then this
chaos happens, and we never had the slightest idea anything
was going on."

"But why would you? He lived over there, and you basically stayed inside. The base is a small, connected
community, but you won't know everyone. You didn't work
with him, or have anything in your lives that caused you to

interact. He was just some stranger you may have passed by on a daily basis, and that was it."

She nodded. "What if that somebody is different than the body who was cremated? What if another person is in that urn? How do you reconcile that, when there could be a whole family grieving who doesn't need to, and another family is looking for a missing loved one, with no clue what may have happened?"

"That's one of those hard questions to answer," he admitted. "Obviously we'll do everything we can to get to the bottom of it."

"Of course if my neighbor faked his death on purpose, he can't access his bank accounts, can't keep his cell phone, and things like that, unless he wants to get caught," Pearl noted. "So how do you trace someone who is trying to hide?"

"Don't worry about it, sweetheart," Gideon replied, with a smirk. "We're on it. We're also picking up some food and going back to my place for dinner."

"I can't. I need to stay here and clean up this mess."

"That's not happening," Gideon noted. "Jasper has the base bringing in a cleaning company."

"I won't argue about that," she muttered, studiously ignoring the mess behind her. "It is not something I ever want to see again. I live and work in the medical field, but I don't deal well with death at this level."

"I understand. It's personal. A gunman entered your home. Your privacy was invaded." Gideon nodded. "I don't know how you feel about it, but we could apply to get you moved to another location."

She stared at him, looked around, gave a tiny shudder that she tried hard to hold back, and nodded. "That might not be a bad idea."

"I think it would be smart," he agreed, with a smile, "but I didn't want to start an application process without talking to you first."

"No reason for me to stay here." She shook her head. "I would have these horrid memories if I do."

"How do you feel about sleeping in this house?"

"Terrible," she muttered. "I feel terrible, but I have to deal with my life again. So it doesn't matter how I feel, does it?"

"You don't have to be strong and stoic all the time," he pointed out.

"I find myself wondering why this didn't bother me so much this morning. We both were dealing with getting rid of all the black fingerprint dust. Yet I was here all that time with Tristan, and, while we didn't focus on it, we didn't specifically avoid it either."

"Honestly, that's one of the reasons I chose him. He's got the personality that can keep someone occupied."

She laughed. "He does have the gift of gab, that's for sure. I guess I was so busy keeping up with what he was saying that I didn't have the time or the energy to look around, or to feel terrible about being here."

"Let's leave this for another day and get you out of here," Gideon suggested. "No reason for you to stay here and feel uncomfortable."

"Maybe so, but it's not as if I have too many options right now," she replied, as she got up. "However, if the cleaning can be done without me, and I can walk back out of here without having to face this right now, that would be lovely."

He led her outside, and she realized that when he meant everybody was leaving, he meant everybody. She glanced again at the house across the road and thought she caught sight of somebody in the window. In a whisper, she asked in earnest, "Has somebody new moved into that house?"

"No, at least not as far as our records show."

"Don't look now but the curtains just twitched."

He stared at her. "Are you sure?"

"As sure as I can be." She shrugged. "I can't just stand here and stare over in that direction, can I?"

"You could," Gideon said, with a smirk, "and you would probably get away with it, but, in our case, not so much."

"If you want me to, I will," she offered. "Just tell me and I'll do it. I'm happy to help in any way I can."

"If you happen to see anything, let me know."

"I already told you that I saw the curtains twitch, but I didn't see a face or anything." She casually glanced around and once again caught the curtain twitch. She nodded at him. "Definitely somebody is in there."

"Good enough." He walked over to talk to Jasper, who was talking to Tristan.

Pearl couldn't hear the conversation, but it was obvious from their heads bent together that the topic was what she had just told Gideon. Tristan nodded and walked down the street, away from the dead guy's house. She wasn't sure what he was doing but figured he would end up checking out the house in question.

Almost as soon as he disappeared, Jasper headed to her and explained, "You'll leave with Gideon, and he will take you to a nice spot so you can pick up some food, and then you'll stay at his place tonight."

She stared at him, then nodded. "How about you just let me walk over to that house, knock on the front door, and see if anybody answers."

He asked, "Do you think anybody will?"

"I don't know," she admitted, with a smile, "but somebody is there, who keeps twitching the curtains, so they are interested in what's going on here. Why don't I just try it?"

And without waiting for him to answer, she turned and headed toward the house in question. She heard Gideon call out to her, but she ignored him, walked straight up to the front door, and rang the doorbell. When no answer came, she knocked several times, then called out, "No point in hiding, I already saw you."

The door slowly opened, and an older woman stood there, staring at her.

"Hello," Pearl said. "Are you related to Drew?"

The woman nodded slowly. "Yes, my brother."

"I'm so sorry for your loss. Are you staying here? I hope you don't t mind my asking. This is base housing and all."

"I know," she said, with an apologetic tone. "I'm just here for a few days, ... figuring out what happened."

"I'm so sorry. It must be so difficult to lose your brother."

"Even more difficult when they tell me that my brother committed suicide, but it so wasn't like him. If they'd told me that he'd been shot, murdered, by some jealous husband, or if one of his shady partners in those get-rich-quick schemes had taken him out, I would have understood, but he wasn't the kind to take his own life."

"Was he involved in anything shady, where somebody might have murdered him and tried to make it look like suicide?"

The older woman had gray hair, was easily in her fifties, looking very tired and sad. She shuddered. "I have no idea. We weren't close, and I'm sure I have no right to even be here," she said, with a wave of her hand. "However, I found the back door unlocked, and I just wanted to come in and get some understanding of his life."

Behind Pearl, Gideon approached, calling out to her.

She smiled and called him over. "I am Pearl, and what's your name?" she asked, turning back to the woman at the door.

"I'm Suzan," she replied, just as Gideon came up behind Pearl.

Pearl introduced Gideon to Suzan. "This is Drew's sister. She just wants to make some sense of what happened, especially since she does not think her brother committed suicide."

Gideon looked at the older woman kindly. "I'm sorry. That's got to be one of the hardest things."

"It is."

"She also just told me that, if Drew had died by a jealous husband or from some crooked deal that he was involved in, it would make far more sense to her than a suicide. She doesn't believe he would have killed himself. I just now asked her if she knew of anything he might have been involved with that could have resulted in someone killing him, then making it look like a suicide."

Gideon addressed Suzan, "Do you?" He spoke with a gentle quality, clearly attempting to put her at ease.

"I honestly didn't have a whole lot to do with my brother's life lately," she shared, looking nervous. "That's why, when the back door wasn't locked, I just came in to try and make sense of it all." Her shoulders started to shake. "How do you reconcile an unexpected death like this?" She had tears in her eyes that she tried hard not to shed. "He appeared to be in good health. He never told me that anything was wrong."

"He may not have wanted you to know either," Pearl suggested. "Men in particular tend to stay quiet when something's terribly wrong in their lives."

"That could be it," Suzan replied, gazing at Pearl with gratitude.

Gideon asked, "Have you had any contact with any of his friends or coworkers or anybody along that line?"

"No, not at all. I paid for the cremation, and I've got his urn at home," she shared, with half a smile. "I followed his instructions, which the lawyer told me that Drew had set out just a few days before, which lent credence to the idea that he committed suicide." She sniffed, holding back the tears again, "I'm just struggling with that whole concept because Drew was always so full of life. So full of plans and ideas, most of which led to trouble. My brother was the guy who always got in and out of trouble. He was always getting involved in shady deals."

Gideon nodded. "I'm an investigator here on base. Can you give me the name of Drew's lawyer?"

She frowned but held up one finger. She returned with her purse and pulled out a card, which she handed over to him.

"Thank you. We'll speak to him. But back to what you said earlier, what kinds of deals was Drew apt to get involved in?" Gideon asked.

"He was always looking for shortcuts to getting rich. He was into shoplifting as a teen and stuff like that. When he went into the military, our parents were grateful because it seemed to be a good answer for him. He got into trouble there too, several times," she added, with a chuckle. "Some-how it never seemed to be so bad that he got seriously punished. Once I thought he was up for a promotion, but, when I didn't hear anything more about it, I asked him about it. He told me that there weren't promotions for guys like him."

"Do you know what he meant by that?"

"I assumed because he had enough things on his record that he wouldn't move up in military rank. I don't know, but honestly, I'm not surprised. What did surprise me after all this time was this whole thing about suicide."

"Exactly," Pearl agreed. "If he didn't commit suicide, the other option is that somebody else killed him and made it look like a suicide. Maybe it was an accident or something that ended up ruled as a suicide."

"Drew left a suicide note with his lawyer, so I don't think anybody was looking at anything other than a suicide in this case."

"No, I imagine not," Pearl murmured. She looked over at Gideon, before addressing Suzan again. "The only other thing I would suggest, and I'm not a counselor, so obviously I can't counsel you on anything, but it's probably not healthy for you to be here."

Suzan slowly nodded.

"Has anybody else come to the door at all?" Gideon asked. "Has anybody asked you any questions about Drew or what happened?"

"No, it's been strangely quiet," Suzan shared. "I hadn't realized how few friends he had. You would think that, if a friend of yours died, you might want to mourn his passing."

Pearl asked, "Usually suicide follows the loss of someone, or financial problems, or mental health diseases. Did Drew have any major issues like that in his life? Did he divorce recently, file for bankruptcy, start seeing a psychiatrist or the like, or had medications prescribed?"

Suzan sighed. "Not that I know of. How sad is it that I don't know more about his life?"

"Maybe," Pearl noted calmly, "but unfortunately, a lot of times, particularly in the case of mental illness, they tend to chase people away from their world, and, by doing so, just reaffirm their ideas that they have no reason for living."

"Also," Gideon added, "if Drew had any health condition or something along that line that he refused to deal with, that's something else that can chase people away. What about his doctor? Have you talked to him at all?" Gideon asked.

"No, it never even occurred to me." Suzan gave her head a shake. "Why didn't it occur to me?"

"That's all right," Gideon said, with a smile. "I can contact his doctor and confirm nothing is there that you should know about."

"Thank you," Suzan said gratefully, as she stepped out onto the front porch. "I still don't even know why the back door was unlocked."

"Was anything disturbed?"

"Not that I know of, and I didn't move anything. I figured that essentially everything here is part of the military housing and all, so nothing's been touched. Although the house is basically empty of Drew's personal effects, it still has furniture. I presume just as it was the day he died."

"Have you seen any estate documents at all?" Pearl asked.

"Yes, more or less. It seems the lawyer must still deal with some things because that's just how probate works, but Drew left behind no money at all. That actually surprises me, and yet"—she laughed—"it doesn't surprise me at all. My brother lived large and didn't particularly care about tomorrow."

Pearl found that interesting because, if he was leaving or had a backup plan to get the hell out of here, then it was quite possible that he had moved a fair bit of money ahead of time. "He may also have given away a lot of his money prior to his death," she suggested. "That's also another sign of someone planning suicide."

Suzan frowned. "I never thought of that, but the lawyer did say some huge transfers had been made in the prior six months, but, when he had talked to my brother, it was all legit."

"Good," Pearl said. "Let's not have any other worries come out of this."

"Exactly." Suzan asked Gideon, "Could you lock up? I don't feel good leaving this wide open."

Gideon immediately nodded. "Yes, of course. And I'll get the housing commission to come over and confirm everything is secured. When you say that nobody's been here, you haven't had anybody come up to the house? You haven't had anybody ask you anything or stop by?

"No," Suzan said, "not today. I did drive by earlier, maybe a week after his death, and I just sat in the car for a long time. That day a couple people went up to the door, banging on it, obviously looking for him. I didn't say anything to them, but they seemed irate that Drew wasn't here."

"And that makes sense too, if they didn't know that Drew had died."

"I felt as if I should say something, but I didn't want to," Suzan shared. "I just wanted to stay out of it all."

"With good reason," Gideon noted. "You didn't recognize the two men, did you?"

She shook her head at that. "No, although one of them was big and burly."

Suddenly Gideon pulled out his phone and brought up a picture of the dead man from Pearl's house and showed it to her. "I don't suppose this would be him, would it?"

Suzan raised her eyebrows and nodded. "Yes, that's him." Then she squinted at the picture and gasped. "Oh dear, is he dead?"

Gideon nodded. "Yes, he died in that house across the street." Gideon pointed to the one across the way.

"Oh, my goodness, do you think he had the wrong house then, and he was looking for my brother's house?" she asked in confusion, looking from one house to the other.

"No, that's my house over there," Pearl noted. "The guy who broke into my house was interested in Drew's house, and he kept staring over at it."

"Oh my," Suzan said. "Now that would make a terrible sense because Drew always had these people around, people you just wouldn't necessarily want your family members to hang out with. Drew kept all those kinds of people around. It was a strange thing about him, but he always had friends that I never quite trusted. So I presume that, when he died, he may have left people in the lurch. Maybe Drew owed them some money or something of that nature," Suzan suggested, still sorrowful, but some anger was there too. She shivered, wrapped her arms around her shoulders, and added, "If that man is dead too, that can't be good either."

"No, it isn't. Yet maybe we'll get a few answers about your brother's death."

She replied with a sad gratefulness. "If you could, I would appreciate it." With that, she walked over to her car and added, "I won't be back. This hasn't been good for me." She sighed. "Even though I was hoping that coming here would give me clarity and would help me find some closure, it feels just the opposite. If anything else, it has just brought up more questions." And, with that, she got into her vehicle and drove away.

Gideon escorted Pearl back to his vehicle. "That was a foolish thing to do," he muttered, as he got her inside.

She smiled and looked over him. "I think your job makes you see shadows in every doorway," she pointed out, with an odd look. "I think there should be a bit of balance."

"Why would you assume it was safe to go up to that door?" he asked, looking at her strangely.

She shrugged. "It seemed like it was a feminine thing to do, to twitch the curtains like that, thinking you're hidden when you're not," she murmured. "I just thought about all the families and friends who were in Drew's life who maybe don't understand what's happening either, so, yes, it was an impulse."

"But it wasn't a smart move, Pearl."

"I get that, and I'm sure you'll wring me out over it. Given the circumstances, it was probably a very foolish thing to do. Yet you and Jasper and Tristan were right here," she explained. "So it turned out okay."

He shook his head at that. "No, it didn't, and we know nothing to prove that."

"If you want to work me over about it, can you wait until we get to your house?" she muttered, holding up a hand, because that was not what she needed right now. "I'm getting tired." Sure enough, she yawned several times.

He stopped at the Italian restaurant to pick up the food he had ordered. When they got to his house, she helped him carry everything in.

"What are you thinking about now?" he asked. "You've been awfully quiet."

She shrugged. "I'm not sure what to make of this whole thing. It just feels so very strange to even think of somebody setting up his own fake suicide."

"Unless he had a reason."

"The reason could easily have been because he was the shooter of your guy, Mason, because Drew was a sniper. Yet it could be because he was afraid of the man who came to my house. And you mentioned Drew was under investigation for gun smuggling. I would lean toward that as probably true enough, just to have the navy checking into that. So faking his death, or even really committing suicide could easily be for just these reasons alone."

"But, if he did fake his death, what are the chances that he's even still alive?"

"Why wouldn't he be? If he faked his death, you would think he had enough skills to potentially get himself out of whatever trouble he got himself into."

"Yet he has some equally skilled people after him, from the navy investigators to these hoodlums who maybe Drew owed money to or the guy who may have hired him to shoot Mason. Drew is company with some heavy-duty bad guys."

"And that all might be true," she admitted. "It just seems that everything is up in the air and that nobody knows what the hell is going on right now. These are all just theories, right? No proof yet?"

He burst out laughing at that. "You got that right."

She helped him sort out the food, then looked at it and asked, "Are you extra hungry? An awful lot of to-go food is here."

"I'm expecting Jasper and Tristan and possibly even Masters to show up," Gideon explained. "This is one of the few places where we can talk confidentially."

"Right, I hadn't considered that," she said. "Do you want me to disappear when they arrive?"

"No, I sure don't," he told her cheerfully, "That's not part of this. Besides, you keep getting yourself into the middle of my investigation, and you do have a perceptive take on things."

"Ha," she snorted. "*I* haven't done anything to get inside your cases. *Other* people are bringing me in, maybe, but I haven't done anything as of yet."

"What do you call this latest little visit you had at Drew's house?"

"It wasn't a problem," she noted, with a smile. "If anything, it helped clarify some things, though still not enough."

"No, not enough," he agreed, "but we'll take the little bits that we get."

Within a few minutes, Jasper showed up with Masters.

She greeted them by saying, "Gideon hasn't killed me yet for knocking on a neighbor's door, so it's probably safe to talk to him."

Gideon groaned. "I wanted to wring your neck, then realized it wouldn't do any good."

"Good, that makes it a little easier on me."

"Although," Gideon pointed out, "you didn't listen or even answer when I called out to you."

"No, I didn't," she confirmed, with a quick look at him. "Sorry about that."

Yet it was obvious that she wasn't terribly sorry at all, and he sighed. "Are you always this disruptive?"

"No, not necessarily," she noted, with a smile in his direction, "but I do think it's important that we sometimes follow our instincts."

"Absolutely," he replied. "It just would be nice if it weren't when people are getting killed."

She winced at that. "Okay, okay, point taken." With that, she looked over at Masters. "Hello. I don't think we've officially met. I'm Pearl."

He smiled. "It's a pleasure," he replied, as he introduced himself. "I'm Masters, one of the other investigators."

"You guys have your own team here, don't you?"

"We're getting there, and we're hoping that, with the extra manpower, we can get ahead of this crime wave, but that's not happening, at least not easily."

"You'll get there," she said, with a careless wave of her hand. "You just have to find out where this Drew guy is."

"But we don't even know that this Drew guy," Masters pointed out, looking at the others, "was Mason's shooter. That is the main case we are all focused on, when not dealing with these side cases that show up in the meantime."

"And yet," Gideon added, "Drew's a sniper, and he's gone missing, and he quite possibly has faked his own death, so that makes him a very good suspect."

"It does, but suspects are just that, *suspects*," Masters replied. "We need something that locks him down into a whole lot-more-than-a-suspect category."

Pearl nodded, as she picked up a plate and served herself. "You'll get there," she said, "and you have my undying gratitude for dealing with Betty."

"Now that," Jasper interjected, "is a seriously sad situation."

"Is there any connection between the lieutenant and Drew's suicide?" she asked suddenly, and silence fell all around for a few moments.

The men shared looks, as Gideon asked, "Why would you even bring that up?"

She looked at them and shrugged. "Why wouldn't I? If Betty was blackmailing the lieutenant, how many other people could Betty be blackmailing over something similar going on, yet not be related to each other?"

The men raised eyebrows at each other, as she shrugged.

"I did ask Gideon today if you wanted to be an investigator," Jasper joked. "I gather that you think we don't know anything and aren't doing anything, but we are."

"Of course you are," she replied. "I would never say otherwise. It's just, like everybody else, it seems we take one step forward and ten steps back."

"Unfortunately that seems to be the nature of this particular investigation into Mason's sniper, and, no, it's not what we want."

Gideon looked over at the other men. "Any recent updates about Drew's life and possible death?"

"Tesla checked in," Jasper replied, with an odd tone, "and the coroner called me back. He went through everything he had, and, short of initially doing a DNA test and having a second person do a physical identification—which, remember, involves a damaged face," he shared, "the coroner would still have made the same determination of suicide."

"Of course. The death was more or less suicide, but is there any chance that it wasn't Drew?" Pearl asked.

"That's why we're waiting for further evidence in order to support that theory, like a DNA match to the military database," Gideon explained. "The coroner's waiting for more as well and is prepared to change his report, if we get evidence to support it. He's also quite angry that something like this could happen, as it's not the world that he generally lives in."

"No, it's not," Pearl agreed. "He works on base and expects a higher degree of honesty and ethics here. That's just what is expected of the navy. That's a fact of life here. Is suicide a little more common on base?"

"It is, unfortunately," Masters stated. "Not everybody is geared for the world of the military," he noted, with a smile in her direction.

Pearl sighed. "I know. I didn't think I would be coming back here myself."

"And yet you did," Gideon muttered, reaching out and squeezing her hand.

She smiled. "That doesn't mean I'm staying though."

"I'm surprised you stayed at all," Jasper noted, "considering the witch you worked with."

"Yeah, and I had to do some deep soul-searching as to why I stayed too," she admitted, with a half laugh. "At the end of the day, I didn't know where else to go."

"So, that's a good thing," Jasper said, "because sometimes your instincts are telling you that it's not the time to go anywhere, that it's just time to stay where you are. Do what you need to do and wait for life to show you the next direction. It sounds to me as if life did."

"Maybe, though I'm not sure I appreciate this direction now."

"Doesn't matter whether you do or not," Gideon said cheerfully. "Life isn't full of answers. It's more full of guidelines."

She chuckled. "I'll go with that too." She finished eating, then looked over at Gideon and said, "If you don't mind, I'll go upstairs."

"I don't mind in the least," he said. "Meanwhile, I'll be down here, as we do have business to talk about."

She nodded. "Good timing for me to go get some sleep."

CHAPTER 13

P EARL WOKE IN the middle of the night, wondering what had disturbed her. She'd heard voices downstairs for what seemed like hours, and then there had been silence. Now she heard footsteps on the stairs, and she froze. Then she recognized the calm assurance of somebody accustomed to the pace and the cadence of climbing these stairs. She smiled. It was Gideon.

When the footsteps hesitated at her room, she called out, "I'm awake."

He opened the door, poked his head in, and asked, "Hey, how come you're awake?"

"I just woke up," she replied, her voice groggy. "I'm not sure what woke me. I assume it was probably you coming up the stairs that popped me awake again," she said, with a smile. "And, no, it's not your fault. It is something I'll probably just have to deal with on a regular basis for a while, after having two intruders."

He nodded. "But you're doing a great job of handling it."

"How did your meeting go?"

"We went over a bunch of information, but we just don't have enough," he said. "There's been no activity on

Drew's credit cards, his bank accounts, passport, nothing."

"If he was into these shady things on a regular basis, he would probably know how to set up a new identity for himself," she suggested.

"We are aware of that," he noted, with a chuckle. "And it's something that we're looking into. Tristan has a few contacts he's already approached, checking to see if somebody with Drew's description got a new identity. We haven't gotten any hits on that yet." He shrugged. "It would be nice to think that we could check the usual transportation hubs, but we don't have the manpower needed to go through all the security camera feeds at all the airports and train stations and bus depots over an unknown period of time and involving an extended range of distance from the base. Plus, Drew still could have simply stolen a vehicle and driven somewhere."

"He also could have just holed up right here, somewhere nearby. There would be absolutely no need for Drew to go anywhere, unless he was afraid of getting caught or of somebody else finding out," she pointed out.

"That's another issue as well," he noted, "and Tesla is already running facial recognition on Drew, restricted to the base and the time since Mason was shot. That might actually uncover something faster than Drew fleeing in another way. All good points, but, *if* Drew *is* responsible for shooting Mason, is he then also responsible for setting up this entire thing, the shooting and the aftermath with these other bad actors? Or did Drew do it strictly for the money, as a hired killer, meaning someone else put him up to it? Then Drew failed to kill Mason, so he would have had to run because there's a penalty to be paid when you don't complete the job."

"What if he didn't want to complete the job? What if killing Mason wasn't the goal? What if Drew was supposed to let Mason live?"

"And there's your soft heart at work again," Gideon noted, with a smile. "Unfortunately the bad guys out there are more inclined to kill."

She shrugged. "I don't know about the soft heart, but, if it were me, and I were being forced to do it, I would make it look like as good of a shot as I could but still miss."

"Yeah, but Mason was shot in the head, which can easily be a deadly injury. He was saved by an inch or so from dying. Yet you think it could have been a forced job for the sniper?"

"Maybe," she said. "It's just a foreign concept to me that somebody would want to intentionally kill somebody like that. It boggles my mind. Besides, to hear you guys talk, everyone loved Mason."

"Not quite everyone," Gideon clarified. "And while killings like this may not show up all the time in your work or your life, they sure do with us. That shit happens all the time."

"True," she murmured, "and I'm not naïve, especially after dealing with Betty. So forcing a sniper to kill someone is a possibility in my mind now."

"It is," Gideon agreed, staring off into the distance.

"And you should get some sleep."

He laughed. "You're right. I should be sleeping," he murmured. "That's where I'm heading right now. I hope to get some shut-eye before something else happens."

"Good."

"I did want to ask you a couple questions though," he said.

"Like what?"

"Are you serious about starting our relationship again? Or at least figuring out if we have something to start again with?"

"I don't know whether we do or not," she murmured, grateful for the darkness of the room to hide her expression, and yet she felt like the shadows wouldn't hide anything. He'd always been extremely good at reading her.

"I don't want to play any games," he stated, as he sat down on the bed with her. "I want to know if you're serious about trying again."

"Yes," she replied immediately. "I am serious, but I have no idea how to make you trust me again. I do realize that I broke that trust. ... And, once broken, trust can be an incredibly hard thing to rebuild."

"It can be," he agreed, "but it can also be something that just takes a little time, then slides into being the norm again."

"That would be lovely," she whispered. "I can't begin to tell you how sorry I am for what I did, but it's been choking me ever since I came back."

"Mason getting shot was horrible, but it brought us together again," Gideon noted. "Even if we don't rekindle what we once had, we've at least found each other as friends again."

"Yes," she agreed, but inside her the bitterness spread. "However, if friendship is all you have left to give, I understand that. Yet I ..." At the last moment her voice broke.

He leaned over and gave her a hug. "I'm not saying that friendship is all I want at all," he clarified, his throat thickening. "Honestly, I think that would be more painful than anything."

Privately she agreed, as she hugged him back. "I don't want to push you into something you're not ready for," she added, "and I understand that it will take some time."

"It wouldn't take that much time," he said. "Do I understand what you did? No. Will I be worried for a while that it might happen again? Possibly." Then he took a moment to add, "But I'm not prepared to spend my entire life worrying about it."

She held her breath as she waited. When he didn't continue, she muttered, "Right now I feel as if you're leaving me hanging, and I don't know what it is you're saying."

He pulled her out of the blankets, until she was sitting in his lap. "What I'm saying is this." And he lowered his head and kissed her.

GIDEON HAD BEEN thinking about Pearl all evening, ever since she went upstairs. He couldn't stand the thought of her alone in the bed, with him down there, but still, this was a business meeting, and he had to keep his head in the game. Once the guys were gone, Gideon figured she was fast asleep and so pushed off going upstairs as long as he could. Leaving her alone had gotten more difficult by the minute. With every step he took up the stairs, he argued that he should not wake her, should give her more time, should let her decide. But his mind argued with him. *Bullshit, get in there, don't give her a chance to change her mind again. Lock this down so you have something to go forward with, and sort it out as you go.*

It would take time before he trusted her fully again. Yet he wanted that chance to see if they still had what they'd had before. It had been wonderful between them back then, and that was one of the reasons he'd had such a hard time when she'd walked. He just couldn't comprehend it. Now he understood it a little bit more, and he had seen how unhappy and how desperate she'd been and what she'd put herself through in order to get near him again. It must have been a hell of a shock for her to discover, after she'd moved back, that he was gone. That she had then stayed and endured all the trouble Betty had dished out was even more amazing.

He couldn't imagine all the torment both he and Pearl had been through over their breakup, and he didn't want any more of that. He just wanted to find peace for everybody, and that meant his taking the first step. She had opened herself up and let him know exactly what she was looking for, but he hadn't made his desires clear, and now he was here to do just that.

He lifted his head and looked down at the tumbled, be-mused look in her eyes and smiled. "That still feels the same."

She nodded, slightly breathless as she whispered, "Absolutely, it feels amazing." She wrapped her arms around his neck, pulled him down, and kissed him, not with passion, but with a tenderness that almost brought tears to his eyes.

He hugged her and just held her close.

"I'm so sorry I hurt you," she whispered.

He placed a finger against her lips. "*Shh*, I know that," he replied, giving her another kiss. "I'm still not sure I understand exactly what happened, what triggered you to leave me without an explanation. Plus, I can't guarantee that I won't bring it up sometimes, like when I'm mad or finding something not going my way. I promise to desperately try not to because it's something that we need to get past as a couple and find that safe ground again," he murmured. "But

I want to try to have a relationship with you again. I want to see if we still have what we had before."

"I hope not," she muttered, crumbling in his arms. When he frowned, she gave him a little smile. "I'm hoping we have something way better, something I'm a little more secure in, less worried about being the wrong person for you, and less worried about our future. As much as I want it to just be us in this relationship," she shared, shaking her head, "we live in a world that's crazy, with a lot of confusion out there. This new relationship will develop over time, but I would like it to be all that we had before, plus a level of confidence in ourselves and each other that brings a new level of peace and safety that I can only imagine at this point."

"I can get behind that," he murmured, as he slowly and tenderly rubbed his nose against hers. He thought about her words and everything that they meant.

"I need you to forgive me, and … I can't even ask for that," she whispered. "All I can do is hope that, over time, you will."

He nodded. "I will. I am. I have," he replied, with a shrug. "One thing I know for sure is that I don't ever want to lose you again." He lowered his head, and this time kissed her with a building passion. When he finally broke away, he was struggling for his breath. "Damn," he muttered.

She nodded. "It's been a long time." He froze and looked down at her, one eyebrow raised. She nodded. "Never anybody for me but you."

He closed his eyes, not even aware how much her answer meant to him until he heard her say it. In the back of his mind he'd still been worried about another man. Somebody better than him, somebody she wanted more, and yet, by her own admission, there hadn't been. He crushed her against him, and then, without even asking, he slid his hands underneath her nightie, over her smooth thighs, along her rounded hip to her belly.

She sucked in her breath, as his hand climbed higher and higher, until he cupped her right breast, and she shuddered against him.

He smiled. "That hasn't changed."

She shuddered again and cried out, making small mewling sounds, as he drew kisses across her neck, down her throat, up against her nightie, before he slipped it over her head and tossed it to the floor. She lay before him completely carefree and happy, her arms opened wide as she waited for him. He quickly shed his clothing, almost tripping as he forgot to first take off his shoes. She chuckled, and he glared at her, but no anger was in his gaze.

"You always used to do that too," she murmured. "You would get so excited that you forgot you still had shoes on."

"I shouldn't even be wearing the damn shoes in the house."

"I thought about reminding you of that, but I figured it wasn't my place."

"It absolutely is your place," he said, with a groan. "I bought this house because I couldn't stand the thought of not having that part of our dream," he murmured. "I can't believe that I finally get a chance to share it with you."

Tears in her eyes, she pulled him down, even as he was still kicking off his socks.

With laughter in his gaze, he happily turned to her, her arms wrapped around him as she kissed him with all the passion that appeared to be pent up inside her. He took the blast full on and felt his own body shuddering in response.

All he could do was hang on for the ride, as she rolled him over to his back and explored the body that she knew so well. Yet it seemed brand-new, a moment to reacquaint herself, as she explored Gideon's familiar body, but better somehow. He hated to see the tears in her eyes, and he wished he could take them away. However, he didn't want to stop whatever was happening between them right now.

She cried out in joy and in pain, for every new wound, every new scar that she didn't recognize or didn't know. He tried to explain, but she placed a finger against his lips, not giving him a chance. Then finally, when she found his erection, he cried out in pain and a joy of his own, as she fully explored the long, hard length of him.

She whispered, "At least this hasn't changed."

He gave a groan and whispered, "How could it possibly, except that it's been dying for you all this time?"

She hadn't asked him further about his prior inconsequential relationships he had already divulged, and that was good because he didn't even want to go there. He hadn't been as good as her, but then he'd had a broken heart to heal. Still, random warm bodies hadn't buried his pain, so he'd quickly stopped. Now as he pulled her into his arms, flipped her on the bed beneath him, and entered her with one final push, she stilled beneath him, slowly wiggling to accept the length, and he realized that she had meant every word of it. She hadn't been out there screwing around with other people, and, for that, he was forever grateful.

Moving slowly and tenderly, he gradually picked up the pace, until she was crying beneath him, screaming at him to bring this to an end. He reached between them and caressed her nub, knowing how sensitive she was there. He often didn't need to do anything other than that. She came apart in his arms, leaving him to drive once, twice, and a third time to his own completion, before collapsing beside her.

She wrapped her arms around him and just held him close. "I'd forgotten but not forgotten," she whispered. "Talk about a homecoming, after such a long time."

He smiled, pulled her tightly to his chest, and muttered, "At least now you're where you belong."

CHAPTER 14

P EARL WOKE THE next morning with an odd sense of disorientation. Then last night's memories flooded back in again. She immediately turned to look beside her, and, sure enough, a naked Gideon slept right next to her. She smiled, half remembering that they had gone from her room to his in the middle of the night because his bed was bigger. She leaned over, kissed him, and then got up and headed to the shower.

The bathroom door opened within a few minutes, as she stood under the hot water. He approached her, staring at her. She smiled and asked, "Are you coming in or staying there?"

He let out a happy sigh. "I just wanted to confirm that this was real." He stepped under the hot water, and they made passionate love all over again.

Her heart brimmed both with tears and with joy. He had had the same morning-after fear that it hadn't been real. She had woken up with a similar sensation. By the time she dressed and made it downstairs for breakfast, she was relaxed and carefree. She walked into the kitchen to find him putting on coffee. She smiled. "Is there even such a thing as people who don't drink coffee in the morning?"

He smiled back at her. "I have met quite a few people who don't drink coffee."

She frowned. "And you still trust them?"

He laughed. "I do, but it will always be something that amazes me because coffee is such an iconic thing to have at breakfast."

"It is for me," she murmured.

"Still?"

She nodded. "It's not as if anything would have changed that." She chuckled. "And some things you just don't change."

"I won't argue with that," he said, "and I can see how you would want coffee first thing in the morning. Some days I don't get my dose of caffeine, but, when I can," he noted, with a satisfied expression on his face, "it's definitely a joy, happiness all around." He picked up the pot of coffee that was done dripping, then poured her a cup, and the two of them sat down at the kitchen table. "So, I have a proposition." She waggled her eyebrows at him, and he chuckled. "Not exactly what I meant," he said, smirking at her. "But given not only the mess but all the drama involving your house, how do you feel about moving in with me?"

She slowly put down her coffee cup and stared at him. "Are you serious?"

"Yes, I am."

He was serious, and the look on his face was calm. "We used to live together, and I figured that the sooner we get back to whatever our new normal will be, the better."

"Are you sure? As you mentioned before, I can get another housing assignment."

"Honestly, it's got nothing to do with your house. It's ... it's what I want. What do you say?"

She smiled at that, feeling the tears choke the back of her throat, and immediately nodded. "Oh, it's definitely what I want. I just didn't want to push it."

"Of course you didn't," he said, with a chuckle. "I didn't want to push you either."

"Push away," she said, with a wave of her hand. "We've missed so many years already that I just want to play catch up."

"And yet, like you, I don't want to play catch up. I want to build something better."

"Yes," she agreed, sitting there, thinking about how this was a perfect end to a perfect night. Yet it was probably on the early side for them to already be on the same page, after only this long.

His phone rang just then, and he checked out who it was and motioned at her. "I have to take this." He got up and walked into the other room.

She hadn't fully explored his house, but she was happy for him because it was such a beautiful place. He'd made a good attempt at making it his. As she sat and waited for him, she sipped her coffee, wondering about the process to get moved in now.

She did need to give notice to her landlord. Did she need to tell the owner that somebody was murdered in his house? Was that her place, or would the base or the MPs, or whoever took care of those kinds of notifications? That would cause her all kinds of chaos, she was sure. She also had to decide when she was going back to work.

It was Friday already, so she still had the weekend to decide, but she should be seriously thinking about going back on Monday. She didn't have unlimited funds, even with the investments from her inheritance, and still needed the job to keep herself afloat, even more so if she would move in with Gideon because she didn't want to be financially dependent on him. She'd always had a problem with being dependent on anybody, and that hadn't changed over the years. She'd become even more independent in many ways, and she couldn't help but think that was a good thing. Still, she didn't want to set off any arguments right now with Gideon.

When he walked back in and sat down, he had a perplexed expression on his face.

"So, are you allowed to tell me what's up?"

He shrugged. "To some degree I could. However, we're not exactly getting anywhere yet. We've found no sign of our Drew guy, still no draws on his bank accounts, credit cards, nothing. The lawyer says that he'd come in, appeared sad and downcast, had made several changes to his estate planning documents, and explained that he'd given away a lot of his money earlier. It hadn't occurred to the lawyer at the time that Drew might be suicidal, and he's beating himself up over it now. Back then it had just seemed like he was temporarily upset, but Drew quickly got over it, and they took care of their business, and Drew went on his way."

"What did the lawyer miss during their last meeting?"

"Now the lawyer's wondering about that, recalling the details of their visit, but, so far, nothing is shaking loose."

"Or not what he might have missed, as much as what his client was planning."

"Exactly. I do have to go to my office, so what will we do with you?" At that, a knock came at the door. When he got up to open it, Tristan came in.

"There's your answer," she said, with a sigh, "as if you didn't already know."

Tristan feigned an overly hurt expression.

She smiled. "If I must have somebody following me around, I'm happy to have it be you," she told him. "But this shadowy prisoner life isn't exactly fun for anybody."

"No, it sure isn't," Tristan agreed, with a smile in her direction. "Even for those of us in the shadowy world with you."

"Which is why it would be nice if there were another solution."

"There is," he declared. "We'll get this thing dealt with, and then I won't have to be here anymore."

She looked over at Gideon. "You'll go to your office then, so Tristan can come with me to my house, right?"

Gideon frowned. "What do you want to do at your house? I don't think the cleaners have been there yet, but it should be handled today."

"I understand that. I just thought that maybe … I was thinking about picking up a few more things."

Gideon smiled. "That's a good idea." He turned to Tristan. "She's moving in here with me. So anything she wants to bring, can you help her pack up?"

He groaned. "I am so not moving-guy material. That's got to be my worst job in the world."

"Sorry, Tristan," Pearl replied cheerfully, "but every assignment has its pros and cons. Lucky for you, I don't have that much stuff. So, yeah, you'll have to help me pack and move my stuff." He mock-glared at her, and she chuckled. "On the other hand, I'll take you out for lunch, if you do good work."

Immediately he clutched a hand to his chest. "Oh, be still, my beating heart. If I work my ass off all day, she'll take me out for one meal." Then he looked over at Gideon, cocked an eyebrow, and asked in a curious tone, "Unless that'll make he-man here jealous?"

Gideon laughed. "Nope, but she's got to eat, and, therefore, you get to go with her."

Tristan shook his head at that. "You guys are too much," he muttered. "Have you got boxes at least? Have you got anything?"

"I've got a few," she said, frowning.

Gideon stood up and told Tristan, "Check out my garage. Should be some out there. I don't know how much Pearl has to move."

She shrugged. "I don't think there's all that much, but I have quite a bit of kitchen stuff."

"Right." He stared at her with amusement. "I forgot about how much you like your kitchen gadgets."

She rolled her eyes at that. "Hey, take me, take my kitchen gadgets."

"Got it. I survived it all before. I don't think it will present a problem now." He got up abruptly and took Tristan out to the garage.

She stood in the open doorway, as they found a bunch of compacted boxes and some packing tape. Very soon Gideon was in his vehicle, ready to hit the garage door button. But then he looked back at her, shut off the engine, and approached her to give her a hard kiss. "Behave yourself." And, with that, he was gone.

She shook her head at his abrupt disappearance, then looked over to see a grinning Tristan. "Glad you find it amusing."

"Hey, I've known Gideon for a long time. This is a good thing."

"Agreed. But this," she added, twirling her finger around

the area, "still feels like I'm being babysat. It's not as if the first intruder wanted me. He was just after the view from my house. And someone still may be watching that house, if Drew is alive."

"Yep. Now we at least know why the gunman had taken over your house. So that's all good too."

"Maybe, it's just so very strange that we haven't gotten any further with it."

"No, not yet. These things take time."

"Maybe so, but, if Drew is Mason's sniper, it would make more sense to take him out after the botched hit, than to let him run free."

"Who says that hasn't happened?" he asked. "Yet we did check with the morgue as to that theory."

She nodded slowly, thinking back to the sister they had met yesterday.

"Now, if you're ready," Tristan began, "let's go take care of whatever we need to pick up from your place."

She smiled. "Okay. I know it's not your favorite thing, but I do appreciate the help."

"I bet you do," he muttered, groaning. "How come every damn body just wants me for my muscles?"

She laughed as she got into his vehicle. "Maybe because you have more muscles than anything else."

"Hey, hey, hey," he cried out in protest, as they drove away. "You better be nice to me. Otherwise I won't pack up your house."

"Oh, good point," she noted immediately. "In that case, no insults—until the job is complete."

And with continuous bickering shared back and forth, they drove the relatively short distance over to her place. When they saw that the cleaners were here, he looked over at her. "Do you want to wait?"

"No, I want to get this done." And she did. She wanted to start fresh with Gideon, and she certainly didn't want to stay here in this house any longer than necessary. As she walked up to the front door, she admitted, "This is one of the hardest stages," she murmured. "You're not sure, but you're sure, and you're excited, but you're scared."

He nodded. "But you lived with him before, right?"

"I did," she said, with a smile. "However, remember how I'm the one who walked away."

"This time you won't," Tristan declared, with a certainty that had her wondering what he knew about her. "So it's all good." As they walked into the house, he showed his credentials to the cleaners, who just nodded at them and continued their work. Pearl and Tristan avoided that area, and she led the way upstairs to her bedroom.

As he looked around the room, he noted, "Wow, you were right. You don't have much, do you?"

"Nope, I sure don't," she agreed, with a smile. "We already took a big load of clothes and personal items over the first day."

He nodded, and they got busy packing. By the time they had the bulk of it done, she looked around and frowned. "I didn't have much, did I?"

"Honestly, you had a surprisingly small amount of personal effects." He studied her curiously. "Was that because you didn't think you were staying?"

"Probably. I came out West without very much because I knew it was a gamble. I didn't collect anything more in the meantime either. You don't collect if you're not staying."

He nodded. "That's very true, but now you *are* staying," he declared. "So it's definitely time to fill his house with your kitchen stuff."

She chuckled. "More stuff is there for sure." It took much longer, once they were in the kitchen to pack it up, than her bedroom had. When she turned around, she noted that the cleaners were gone, and it was just the two of them. She sighed. "We've pretty well got this beat."

He groaned in an exaggerated way. "Damn good thing," he muttered. "You've busted all my muscles."

She snorted. "If that's the case, they weren't all that good to start with."

He flashed her a bright, mocking grin and nodded. "I'll take these outside and get them all loaded up in my truck. You figure out what else you want, and we'll go from there."

She checked her watch and realized it was almost noon. "At least the cleaners are done."

"Yeah, it's just us now." With that, he started moving boxes into the garage. His truck was parked outside on the driveway, but it would shorten the distance and cut out turns and inner doorways. She finished filling the box she was on and then worked on filling the next one. Noting an odd sensation, she turned around to see her back door open, and Suzan, Drew's sister from across the street, stood there.

"Hey," Pearl said, with a bright, welcoming smile. "You decided to come back after all. Was that wise, with bad guys looking for your brother?"

Suzan shrugged. "Hard to stay away."

Yet Pearl noted something slightly different in her tone. "Are you all right?" she asked in concern, "It's got to be hard dealing with the loss of Drew, especially if he was the last of your family."

"The cleaners, … they were working here at this house, weren't they?"

She winced. "Yeah, they sure were."

"Is this where the guy was killed? I heard something about it on the news, and then it was mentioned yesterday."

"I don't remember if it was mentioned or not," Pearl clarified, "but, yes, the intruder was killed here." She wasn't sure it was mentioned on the news either.

Suzan nodded slowly. "Did you know the guy?"

"No, I didn't. He was watching your brother's house. At least that's what he told my friend."

"Your friend talked to the intruder?" Suzan asked.

At that, Pearl nodded. "Not a whole lot of choice when he was being held at gunpoint."

Suzan gave a shudder. "That sounds terrible. I can't imagine my brother being mixed up in something like that."

"Maybe not, but just remember whatever good memories that you have of Drew. Don't worry about the intruder at this point."

"Is it so easy though?" Suzan asked, staring at her. "You're obviously moving. Where are you going?"

For whatever reason, Pearl felt almost too much of a question was there.

Suzan softened her tone immediately, then backed off, as if she were unsure how her questions had been received. "Not prying," Suzan added, far too quickly. "I guess I'm just surprised."

"I'm not sure where I'm going at the moment, but I have to go somewhere, at least temporarily," Pearl hedged. "A man was killed in this house. I don't want to stick around and have those memories going around in my head again and again."

"No. I'm sorry. That would be awful." She looked at the kitchen and smiled. "Obviously you haven't been here all that long."

"Yet I have been. I just hadn't unpacked a lot of things, and I didn't get all that comfortable here." Suzan didn't say anything. "Is there something I can do for you? Otherwise, sorry, I'm busy, trying to stay on schedule here."

"I can see that," Suzan replied, then nodded, as she turned and looked toward the open door connecting to the garage. "You're just stacking up boxes in the garage? That seems like an odd thing to do."

Pearl turned and saw one of the boxes in the garage that still hadn't been loaded on Tristan's truck. "It's the easiest way to get things from here to there." Suzan just nodded again. Awkwardly Pearl repeated, "I'm sorry, but I do need to get back to packing."

"Of course, of course," Suzan muttered. "I'm sorry. You were so friendly yesterday."

Almost immediately Pearl regretted being so friendly but knew that wasn't the right attitude either, especially since the woman had just lost her brother. "I'm sorry, and you're right. It's a tough time for you. Maybe you should get some counseling."

"Maybe. Did you ever see what was going on over at my brother's house?" she asked, turning to stare through a nearby window. "Would you mind if I took a look from the living room to see?"

"There's really nothing you can see," Pearl said. Yet she walked Suzan through to the living room. "Still, you're welcome to take a look."

"Thank you, and you're right. Not a whole lot to see, is there?"

"No, there sure isn't." Pearl smiled.

"And you never saw anything?"

"No, I never saw anything. I don't know why the intruder thought this place might have something of a view, but I'm sorry to say the intruder lost his life because of it."

"Did you kill him?" Suzan asked in shocked fascination.

"No, no, God no," Pearl cried out. "That would have been a lot harder to deal with. No, it was one of the men who came to rescue me."

"Rescue?" Suzan asked in an odd tone.

"Yes, rescue," Pearl declared. "Remember how this strange man was inside my house, and he had a gun, and I was just outside?"

Suzan nodded, as she stared in fascination across at the other house. "How is it that, after living here for months, you never saw my brother over there?" she asked, turning to look at her in confusion.

"Because I've never been the type to sit and watch the neighbors out my windows," she replied, realizing the time she was wasting. Pearl pointed toward her kitchen and, as politely as she could, said, "I do need to finish packing."

"Of course, of course." Suzan smiled. Then she turned and headed to the back door, the same way she had come inside. At the door, she looked back. "Thank you for your kindness yesterday." With that, she quickly walked outside.

Pearl felt bad because she'd essentially pushed Suzan out the door. Yet Pearl quickly finished packing up a box, and then realized Tristan hadn't come back inside for quite some time. She stepped into the garage and called out, "Tristan, are you here?"

Nothing, no answer, not a sound came. Frowning, she headed outside to his vehicle parked in the driveway, looking for him. When she still saw no sign of him, she called out again, "Tristan, where are you?"

Getting worried, she raced back inside and searched everywhere she could, then headed back outside. She stopped to consider what could have happened and noted how Suzan had come over. With that thought now paramount in her mind, she quickly phoned Gideon. When he answered, his tone was distant, as if she'd pulled him out of a meeting.

"I don't know where Tristan is," she cried out immediately.

"What? What do you mean, you don't know where he is?"

"I don't know where he is," she repeated. "The neighbor came by, and I was talking to Suzan for a few minutes, and then I went to find Tristan, and I don't see him," she explained. "He's not in his vehicle or in the garage. He went out to load stuff in his truck, while I packed up things in the kitchen, but there's no sign of him."

"Whoa, whoa, slow down," he stated calmly. "I'm on my way. When did you last see him?"

She paused for a moment. "At least fifteen or twenty minutes ago," she muttered, fear now creeping into her tone. "Did something happen to him because he was here with me?"

"Don't even go there," Gideon said. "We're already on the way to you. You mentioned the neighbor."

"Yeah, the woman who we spoke with yesterday. The sister of Drew Honeycutt, Suzan."

"Right. Okay, we'll be there as fast as we can. Give us five minutes. Stay in the house, lock the doors, and don't go outside. Do you hear me?"

"Why though? I need to find Tristan."

"We'll find him. ... I promise. We'll find him."

Even as she stood here sputtering and refining her argument, she heard vehicles pulling up outside. She raced out to the front yard.

"Any sign of him?" Jasper asked her, as he and a few guys spilled out of his truck.

"No, I can't find him anywhere."

With that, a group of men split up and took off all around, both inside and outside. Gideon arrived and now raced toward her. "Now, let's go over it again."

As she started to explain, his phone pinged, and he held it up. "I also have a picture I want to show you." He pulled up a photo, a picture of Suzan. "Is this the woman we saw yesterday and you saw this morning?"

"Yes, yes, it was."

He nodded grimly. "Here's the thing. Drew didn't have a sister."

GIDEON CAUGHT PEARL as she collapsed backward, with a wordless cry. He immediately scooped her up in his arms, then carried her into the living room and carefully set her on the couch. "Easy," he said. "Take it easy."

"Tristan," she said in a frenzy. "Did she take Tristan?"

"I don't know that she had anything to do with this, but we're looking for him. Just hold tight. Give us a chance to sort out what's going on. Let's not panic."

She shook her head, just as someone called to Gideon from outside.

She scrambled to her feet, and he pushed her back down on the couch again. "Stay here," he ordered, his tone brooking no argument. She glared at him, and he added, "I need to find out what's going on." He walked to the doorway, quickly spoke to someone, then turned back to her. "They found Tristan. He's alive."

She sank back, tears in her eyes. "Oh, thank God," she muttered, catching her breath.

"It's okay," Gideon said. "Tristan's alive. They are driving him to the hospital."

"Do we know what happened?"

"No, not yet," Gideon noted, with a shake of his head, "but we at least have him."

Jasper joined them almost immediately, took one look at Pearl, and sat down across from her. "I need to hear what happened."

"He headed outside to load up more boxes, and I was still packing up in the kitchen. We'd been joking and teasing all morning, just making it a little bit more bearable. Suddenly this neighbor, not the neighbor but Drew's sister, the woman from last night, Suzan, showed up, and I started talking to her. I didn't even notice that Tristan hadn't come back in again right away because I was focused on her. I didn't hear from him, but I wasn't worried. I had no reason to be worried since he'd been right here with me the whole time."

"Anything specific about Suzan that you remember?"

"She wasn't ... she wasn't quite the same as last night." Pearl frowned. "It was more like she was playing a role this time," she noted, glaring at them. "She was still talking about her brother, but she did ask me if I'd seen anybody across the way. Then asked why I wouldn't have seen anybody. I told her how I'm not the type to sit and stare out windows and watch the neighbors."

"She specifically asked you that?" Gideon and Jasper exchanged a look.

Pearl had no idea what that meant, but she nodded. "Yeah, she did. She just nodded. I told her several times that I needed to get back to packing, and then finally I ushered her out the door. Then I went back to packing, only to realize that I hadn't heard anything from Tristan. So I went looking for him, and you know the rest."

Jasper nodded. "So, the question is whether she's the one who hurt Tristan. He was hit in the back of the head, probably while bent over to pick up something. He was on the far side of his vehicle and had been rolled underneath."

She stared at him and shook her head. "Which could suggest that Suzan probably did it, since she didn't have to lift him."

"It's possible. It's also just an easy way to get somebody out of sight for a little while, not necessarily for a long time. Whoever hit Tristan and stowed him beneath his truck was looking to keep him out of view."

"But if she was after something, why didn't she go after me?"

"Maybe because you didn't know anything or maybe because you'd been kind to her. Maybe because she was keeping you out of harm's way. I don't know," Gideon replied, "but obviously we have to figure it out."

"And Drew *didn't* have a sister?"

Jasper replied, "Correct."

Gideon also nodded. "Exactly. According to the information we just got in this morning, Drew didn't have any family. He was alone, which is one of the reasons people assumed he'd committed suicide, since he didn't have anybody."

She sagged deeper into the couch and stared up at him. "So, Suzan's probably got something to do with this, but why would she be hanging around?"

Gideon suggested, "Because, for one, she may have been in cahoots with Drew, or she could have been lying for him, or could be a part of his fake suicide, or even a part of his alleged gun smuggling. Maybe she was his partner in crime, and he took off without her, not paying her even."

Jasper added, "Or maybe she's one of the bad guys after Drew. Maybe she's the one who hired him and wanted to take him out, after he botched the Mason shooting. Maybe Drew got wind of it and disappeared. There are all kinds of options."

"Exactly," Gideon agreed, "and, once again, we have too many options. If you want, Pearl, we can take a run to the hospital to check on Tristan to know for sure he's okay."

She nodded, as she looked up at him, tears in her eyes. "Yes, let's go. I don't want anybody getting hurt because of me."

"None of this is because of you," he declared. "You know that."

She shook her head. "But it wouldn't have happened if it wasn't for me."

Gideon laughed. "You mean, because you're here packing up, so we can get you moved into my place? No, that doesn't wash. All of this, *all of this* is their fault, not yours," he said. "And, yes, Tristan is awake. So let's go check in with him at the hospital."

"What about this woman, Suzan, or whatever her real name is?"

"Oh, don't worry," Gideon replied, with a careless wave. "Everybody is out looking for her right now."

Pearl nodded. "She acted odd when she was asking me those questions. I didn't so much feel she was being duplicitous, but she was hiding some emotion. But now I'm feeling like she was *involved* with Drew, ... if you know what I mean."

Gideon nodded. "She could have been his partner in crime and his lover as well. That could be true."

"I do want to see Tristan," she said, immediately walking to the door. She turned to face Gideon and declared, "I would just as soon never come back here again."

"Understood." Gideon looped an arm around her shoulders and looked over at Jasper. "She wants to confirm Tristan is okay."

Jasper nodded. "Just remember ..."

"Will do," Gideon replied.

Pearl waited expectantly, but nothing more was said. As they headed to Gideon's truck, she looked over at him and asked, "What did Jasper mean by that?"

"He's reminding me that the Suzan woman is still at large, and we don't know why she came back again today."

"I guess that's the part that confuses me," Pearl murmured. "Did she plan on doing something to me, then saw Tristan, and didn't have enough time to deal with both of us, or decided it was too much? Or maybe she decided I wasn't enough of a danger to her, or didn't know anything?"

"All of the above could potentially be true," Gideon murmured, "and, when we have answers, we'll share what we can tell you. In the meantime, we have no clue."

Pearl groaned. "That's always the worst thing."

"It is," he agreed. "The waiting and finding no answers to our questions are two of the hardest parts of our job."

As they got to the hospital, Pearl frowned. "The only reason for taking Tristan out would be because he might have stopped Suzan from coming inside and talking to me."

"Or he saw her when she was leaving the house, *after* talking to you," he pointed out.

"Right, that could have happened too." Pearl's shoulders slumped. She got out of the vehicle, waited for Gideon to lock it up and then to come around to her.

He wrapped an arm around her shoulders and said, "Let's go have a talk with Tristan and see if he saw anything, and then we'll head back to my place."

"And now all my stuff is half here and half there."

"Don't worry about it. We'll arrange for it all to be delivered to my place." He watched as she just shrugged, as if she didn't give a crap. Right now he could imagine that she wasn't too worried about her personal property.

Pearl changed the subject back to Suzan. "Suzan did ask me if I'd ever seen anybody over at Drew's place. Then she did say something off."

"What was it?" he asked, stopping to face her.

"Just something about *Why wouldn't I have seen it.*"

"Meaning that *anybody* would have seen it?"

"I think so. … I think she was figuring out what I saw, if I saw something that was important or not, but, if I hadn't seen it, why I hadn't seen it. I told her that I didn't have the time or the energy to spend watching my neighbors because I worked and just didn't give a crap."

"Do you think she believed you?"

"I don't know, but she didn't hit me, and she didn't hurt me, so maybe she did believe me. But that would imply that she had a soft spot, and I'm not sure the woman I saw today had any such thing."

"Seeing something at Drew's house could be problematic for her. She may have decided not to hurt you because Tristan was there—or maybe she didn't even know Tristan was there. Maybe having heard you say something, Suzan changed her mind. Regardless, she's quite likely to come back after you."

"But she had an opportunity right then to do whatever to me."

"But yet *not*, as Tristan was there."

"I guess," she muttered. "I guess it's possible that he came back into the garage, and she heard him, then decided to leave. But, if so, after she'd knocked him out, why didn't she come back inside to hurt me or take me or whatever?"

He smiled and shook his head. "Maybe somebody saw her hit Tristan. And we're still canvassing the neighborhood for that info."

"Right." Pearl groaned. "She knocked him out, but is she coming back after Tristan too?"

He tucked her closer to him and whispered, "Let us worry about that."

"I don't want anybody hurt because of me," she repeated.

He smiled. "I understand the sentiment, but not your guilt."

She paled and nodded. "Not to mention the fact that somebody died at my place."

"And that was not your fault either."

"I appreciate that you were protecting me, but damn it. ... I just want all this to stop."

"You and me both," he declared.

They walked inside the emergency room, and she heard hollering from somebody within one of the curtained exam rooms.

She immediately yelled, "Tristan, stop that!"

Silence came, and a nurse poked her head around the

curtain, with a big grin on her face. "That shut him up."

Pearl stepped through Tristan's curtain and glared at him. "What are you doing, making all that ruckus?" He glared at her, and she shook her head. "No, enough hollering. I had to confirm you were okay."

He flashed her a bright grin. "See? I told you that you would fall in love with me."

She snorted. "Yeah, no, so not happening. As you already know perfectly well, this guy beside me is mine."

"Yeah," Tristan muttered, with a sad look, "but I could always hope."

"Oh please, you would run a million miles away if you thought I might take you up on that offer."

He waggled his eyebrows. "But you don't know that for sure."

CHAPTER 15

T HE WHOLE TIME they bickered and teased, Pearl studied Tristan's features intently. "You can't be that badly hurt if you're still arguing with me," she declared, crossing her arms over her chest.

"Exactly. I'm not badly hurt. See? That's total proof." He glared at the nurse behind Pearl. "She won't let me go until a doctor sees me."

"Of course she won't," she told Tristan. "That's her job, and you won't get her in trouble just because you didn't do your job." He opened his mouth and glared at Pearl now, and she grinned. "Gotcha."

Tristan shook his head. "Did Suzan hurt you?"

"No, she didn't hurt me," Pearl said, "and I knew you would be upset about that, but, no, she didn't hurt me. She didn't do anything to me. I talked to her and had no idea that she'd knocked you out, until I couldn't find you after she left, and so I called for help. Did you see her attacking you?"

"Just coming up behind me," he confirmed. "I turned and ended up with a partial blow to the head, which is probably why I'm still alive."

"But she managed to roll you under the vehicle."

"Yeah, that part will never leave me alone." He growled. "I don't understand why she came back today though."

"She is not Drew's sister," Gideon began, as he stepped up beside Tristan, "because Drew doesn't have a sister. So that leads to other reasons why Suzan would come back today, for example, maybe she thinks Drew is still alive too."

Tristan stared at him in shock and then slowly nodded. "Now that makes more sense. So why else would she come back?" He looked over at Pearl. "Any ideas?"

"Not really, except for Suzan asking outright if I knew anything, from watching out the window at Drew's place, which I told her wasn't my style. Yet she seemed to be a little more upset about the guy who was killed in my place than about Drew dying." She took a moment to consider. "*That* may well be why she was there. She did ask me if I was the one who killed my intruder, but I told her no. It was the men coming to rescue me. She was a little bit upset about that."

"Maybe she knew the intruder," Tristan noted.

Gideon suggested, "Maybe *the intruder* was her brother because I sure as hell can't see that gunman having a romantic partner like Suzan, but you never know with women," he admitted, giving a wave of his hand. "Anyway, we have everybody out looking for Suzan right now."

"If she was supposed to kill you"—Tristan pointed at Pearl—"that failure will cost her."

"Not if she's part of this, one of the ringleaders," Gideon stated, with a forceful tone.

Tristan shook his head. "I don't see her as a mastermind. That woman has a boss she reports to. I see her more as a liability now. That's why she was talking to Pearl, getting answers. If Suzan was supposed to do a job and didn't do it, it doesn't matter who she's sleeping with or how she's a part of this. She's now done something that the bosses can't allow to continue."

"Maybe," Gideon replied, "but, if she can convince them that she had nothing to do with it, she should be safe."

"I don't trust it though," Tristan murmured, as he turned to Gideon. "Would you trust her if you had some doubts?"

Gideon immediately shook his head. "No, I sure wouldn't." He stared off into the distance. "We just need to find her."

"You'll find her dead," Tristan snapped. "She'll turn up in a dumpster somewhere, probably killed soon after she left Pearl's place."

"If that's the case," Pearl asked, "why didn't somebody go dump her body and then finish you off?"

"Maybe because, once he realized what she'd done and how public it was, he decided to get rid of her first, and maybe I was to be next," Tristan suggested, with a shrug. "Maybe he was hoping I would still be there. Maybe he was hoping all kinds of things that didn't come to pass, but I can tell you one thing for sure. So far this group hasn't allowed anybody to fail, and that's what she just did, soft heart or not. Suzan let Pearl walk, and Suzan left me alive. Both of those things will be a black mark against her."

Gideon's phone rang just then, so he excused himself and stepped outside of the curtain barrier. Pearl walked closer to Tristan and asked, "So, how are you feeling?"

"Like I got slammed over the head," he said bluntly.

She smiled. "That's the correct answer, as that is exactly what happened."

He groaned. "And she just talked to you? *Just* talked?"

"She *just* talked to me, and I didn't even realize we had a problem, not until she was gone. I'm so sorry. I should have gone out there looking for you sooner."

He shook his head. "No, I let my guard down. I was packing up those damn boxes."

She winced. "Seems like those damn boxes are causing nothing but trouble."

He nodded. "You should just get rid of it all."

"I might at this point, because who needs more of this headache?" She sat here and visited with him, making sure that he felt okay, convincing him that he needed to stay long enough for the doctor to check on him.

He asked her, "Have you been in the ER lately? Do you know how long I've been waiting already?"

"Somebody will be here soon," Pearl assured him.

Just then a nurse stepped in, and a doctor followed. "Are you his wife?"

"No, I am the person he was protecting when he was attacked." At that, the doctor's eyebrows shot up. He was about to say something, and Pearl declared with a finality that was hard to argue with, "Don't bother telling me to leave. I'm here and I'm staying."

Rolling his eyes, the doc nodded. "I've come to learn that some women are just not worth arguing with."

"Good," she said, with a smile.

Just then Gideon stepped in behind her, and the doctor glared at him now, until Gideon said in an apologetic tone, "I'm taking her with me."

"Good," Tristan said. As Gideon turned to leave, Tristan swung his legs over the hospital bed. "Wait, wait, wait. Let me come too."

The doctor shook his head. "You are staying here for at

least a few minutes, while I sort you out."

Gideon pulled Pearl through the curtain and whispered, "One, Tristan should be checked over, and you'll be in the way, and, two, we just found Suzan."

"Where?"

"She's coming in via ambulance. She's been shot, and I'm not sure she'll make it."

Pearl stared at him and swallowed hard. "So, Tristan was right."

"Looks like it." Gideon nodded. "I'm hoping that, when she arrives, she's verbal, but I don't know that yet. If she's got life-threatening injuries, they won't let me talk to her anyway."

Pearl winced and nodded. And, sure enough, the ambulance pulled up within a few minutes, and the EMTs ran in with a patient. Then the doc and the nurse in with Tristan all rushed out to help in the ER with the new arrival. All kinds of chaos broke loose as the emergency doctors and nurses jumped in to save her.

From the sidelines in the hallway, Pearl stared into the emergency room, just out of the way, but it was hard to see what was going on, except that it was obvious the poor woman was in desperate straits. At one point in time, Pearl looked over at Gideon and whispered, "It doesn't look like she'll make it."

"We have to trust the doctors," Gideon said, but his tone was tight with worry. Pearl knew what he was thinking. He was worried they were about to lose their one potential lead. As it was, the doctors eased back a little bit when they got Suzan's blood pressure and pulse under control. She was conscious for only a moment. She looked around, struggled to sit up, and, in the midst of her struggle, Gideon stepped forward to talk to her, but Suzan's gaze landed on Pearl.

Suzan took one look at him, then at her, and her eyes widened and she cried out, "Run." She gave a half guttural sound and fell back.

The doctor hollered for a crash cart, but they could do nothing more. "She is gone."

CHAPTER 16

E VERYBODY TRIED TO figure out just what had happened and whether Suzan's message to run was directed at Gideon or directed at Pearl. She turned to Gideon. "Don't ask me. I don't have an answer for you." When his phone rang a few minutes later, he spoke to somebody briefly.

When he ended the call, she stared at him and said, "I'm not sure I even want to know what that call was about."

He stared down at his phone, then at her. "I have to go talk to the coroner."

"Why?" she asked.

"Because he has a body, one that he told me bears a striking resemblance to Drew, the man who supposedly committed suicide."

Her shoulders sagged, as she realized they probably had yet another murder on their hands. "Will this ever stop?" she whispered, rubbing her arms.

"It will," Gideon declared, "but it's likely to get much uglier first, before it gets better."

Jasper joined them in Tristan's curtained ER room, then told Gideon, "Let's get going."

The two of them quickly headed to the morgue, leaving Pearl alone in the curtained ER room beside Tristan. When she filled him in on the little bit Gideon had shared, Tristan's eyebrows shot up. "Now that's an interesting twist."

"If that wasn't Drew's sister, and yet she was looking for Drew, why would they have killed both of them?"

"A double-cross," Tristan said immediately. "That would be my take."

"But that also means that, by taking out both of them, we'll have no leads on anybody," she noted, "and we're right back at the beginning."

"Not at all," Tristan countered. "As a matter of fact, every time the bad guys take out somebody, they give us a whole lot more links to work on. Everybody has relationships with somebody, and, in this case, we now know about a relationship between Drew and Suzan, two people who were supposedly brother and sister, and some connection with at least Gideon, if not somebody else in our group, like you. We're getting there. It doesn't seem like it, but we are."

"It doesn't seem like it at all," she claimed. "On the other hand, the gunman involved in my home invasion and Drew's fake sister may have known each other, yet another connection, and both of them are dead now. Plus, if Drew was Mason's sniper, he's dead as well."

Tristan smiled. "You should feel better then, so nobody will be coming after you."

She hesitated. "Do you think that's true?"

"I do," Tristan declared, with a nod. "For whatever reason they *were* interested in you. However, now with your intruder and Suzan both dead, both of the people most directly involved with you, I think the ringleaders are also over and done with you. So you get to relax now."

"It doesn't feel like it," Pearl muttered, "The one guy who had been in my house, he is dead but he may have had a partner."

"Now that could be true too," Tristan noted, his eyes widening, "I wonder what happened to him."

When an odd *click* sounded behind her, Pearl stiffened.

Tristan's eyes widened, and he grabbed her hand.

"Isn't that sweet?" The man behind her spoke in a deep, raspy voice. "Whoever yells out for help, I'm shooting the other one of you. You're right. Everybody is dead," he shared. "Whether we wanted to kill them or not, we had to because we can't have witnesses. Once you leave those holes open to leaks, you can never close them otherwise."

She slowly turned, and, and sure enough, it was the second guy she had seen walking in her neighborhood.

He nodded at her and smiled. "You recognize me, even though I was just outside on the street on the day my buddy was in your house."

"You were there at the same time as Betty."

"Yeah, that crazy loon of a woman." He smiled. "She asked me which house was yours, and I told her." He shook his head. "I couldn't even figure out what she was doing, leaving a package on your front porch, but it was bad, whatever it was. It stunk. I didn't need anybody to tell me that whatever was in that bag was urine, maybe mixed with poop."

She nodded slowly. "So, why are you here now?"

"You don't need me to tell you that either. You just need to know that we're cleaning up some of the mess."

"Did that woman need to die?"

"Yeah, she left you alive, and she didn't kill this guy," he said, with a smirk. "Failure is not an option, at least not for the boss."

"Who is the boss?" she asked. "Who is behind all this?"

He smiled gruesomely. "It doesn't matter."

"It does matter because this is all about Mason," she said. "All of it is connected to him."

He narrowed his gaze, as if seeing Pearl for the first time, now assessing and weighing his options. "You are getting too smart for your own good."

"It doesn't take much brains to figure this out," she replied. "I don't understand why you guys seem to think that we won't understand what's happening here. I just don't get why anybody is after Mason. By all accounts, that man has been good to so many people. Thousands of people, maybe tens of thousands, are all very dedicated to him."

The gunman shook his head. "Me? ... I'm just a contractor, I don't give a shit why this guy hates Mason, but I can tell you that he does, and that's good enough for me. He's paying for all this."

"Yet wasn't it Drew who shot Mason?"

"Yes, Drew was the hired gun," the man confirmed, surprised. "Why the hell do you even know all this?" He spoke a bit more harshly now, "Besides, Drew is gone, so nobody knows anything anyway."

"We know that your boss had Drew killed. Maybe you should be worried about that event too," she suggested. "Yet you're still working for the boss, cleaning up all the messes. Why?"

"Because it's what I do." He smirked. "You hire a cleaner, ... you get a cleaner."

She stared at him. "Oh my God, you were one of the cleaners in my house."

He nodded. "Yeah, that's right. I was in there cleaning up the blood left behind by my buddy," he said, with a headshake. "Can't say I saw that one coming. Yet I saw

Suzan coming. I saw her coming, I was sent to watch her do her job, and instead I watched her fail. So I took care of her before anybody else got wind of it."

"You kill your own people?"

"It's bad for business when you can't do your one job."

"Did you hire Suzan?" Pearl asked curiously. "Do you hire people who are no good at it?"

"No, I don't normally." He glared at her. "Thanks for the reminder, but, in this case, I needed a local."

"What was her relationship to Drew?"

"They were lovers, but Drew was running out on her. He took the money and ran, so she wasn't there to kill you. She was there to figure out what you knew. She thought maybe you were the other woman."

"Jeez." Pearl frowned at him. "I didn't even know Drew."

"And she ended up believing you, but the trouble was, she exposed herself. She made herself visible, and that we couldn't have. Then she knocks a military investigator over the head," he added, with a careless wave at Tristan. "but why she didn't take him out, who knows? Who does that?"

"That's like asking who comes into a hospital and attacks somebody, even knowing the place is full of people," Pearl pointed out. "Who does that?" She watched the curtain behind the gunman shift ever-so-slightly. "How is it you expect to get away with this?"

"Oh, that's easy." He pointed at the white doctor's coat he wore. "Everybody looks for a doctor and expects to see a doctor wearing a lab coat. So, when they see this getup, it doesn't matter whether you're a doctor or not. You can get away with all kinds of shit."

At that, she smiled. "So that answers another question, I

guess. You're the one who tried to kill Mason in his hospital room. And you're the one who tried to kidnap Sebastian."

He stared at her, but now his gaze was no longer friendly. Hard-as-ice glints lit his gaze. "Now, you weren't supposed to know that."

"Why? Because you failed there, both times, didn't you? I suppose the powers above you would love to know about that."

"You've got a mouth on you, don't you?" He spoke in a conversational tone, as he shifted, looking at Tristan and then back at her, just now twisting a silencer on his handgun.

She knew he was about to make a move, and she was desperate to stop him, but she and Tristan were at a definite disadvantage right now. She figured Gideon was on the other side of the curtain, and she would trust him.

When the gunman suddenly raised his gun, and she heard a single *pop*, she instantly closed her eyes against the incoming pain. Yet none came. She opened her eyes to see the gunman slump onto the ground.

She looked down at Tristan, pulling his hand out from under the covers, revealing his gun, having shot right through the sheets.

He looked over at her and smiled. "See? I can still do my job."

She leaned over and gave him a hug, as both Jasper and Gideon stepped in.

Gideon walked over, wrapped his arm around her and just held her close.

She asked him, "Were you there behind the curtain?"

"Yes, just in case," he muttered, with worry in his gaze. "I waited for Tristan to make his move. Don't worry. You wouldn't have been shot either way."

"Says you." She groaned. "Christ, what a mess."

"Maybe, but you got the gunman talking," Jasper noted, looking over at her, "and that is huge. We know a lot more than we did."

"Maybe," Pearl said, "but what we still don't know is who is behind it all."

Jasper shrugged. "No, but we had lots of theories confirmed today. We now know Drew was the sniper. We know who was cleaning up all these bodies, our dead cleaner here on the floor. And we know why Suzan came to you. We also know Drew faked his suicide, so he could run. Yet the cleaner killed Drew as well."

Gideon added, "There are a lot of connections and people involved that we have answers for, and that's huge." Gideon pulled her close and whispered, "You are damn good at this."

"I still don't want a job like yours," she stated, with a headshake. "I think I'll stay on the outside and work as a consultant instead."

Gideon burst out laughing.

Even Jasper grinned at her. "Not a bad idea." He smiled. "Now, do you want to finish packing up at your place and get moved to his? I'll come over later, after we get this mess cleaned up." He turned to Gideon.

"You're not leaving me here," Tristan declared. "I'm coming too. Jeez, do you know how many people die in this place?" And, with a grin, he sat up and tossed off the covers, as he held out his gun to Jasper. "I suppose you'll want this too."

"You better keep it for now. And we will file an investigation into this death," he added, "but it was a clean shooting in front of witnesses. If you hadn't pulled the trigger, Gideon or I would have."

"Next time feel free," Tristan suggested. "It seems I've been popping a lot of people lately."

"Hey, it goes with the job. Head back over with them and try and keep them safe, will you?" Jasper told Tristan.

"That's not fair," she cried out. "Tristan's hurt."

"Good." Jasper looked at her. "In that case, Pearl, you keep Tristan safe, and, Gideon, look after them both. I'll stay behind and deal with the authorities."

She laughed, turning to face Gideon. "Not everything is loaded in Tristan's truck, but I think the rest of my personal effects are pretty-well packed up."

"Good, if you're up for it, let's go finish the job, and we'll talk to Jasper later." And, with that, the three of them quickly made their escape, before all the authorities raced inside, not to mention Tristan's doctor.

Outside in the parking lot, she looked at Tristan. "I still think you're running away from the doctor and should stay in the hospital for a bit longer."

"Damn right I'm running," he said. "Do you know how much paperwork I have ahead of me now? And the place will be swarming in a matter of minutes with authorities wanting to talk to me, over and over again."

She winced as she thought about it. "I imagine it's all pretty rough, isn't it, filling out all those reports, defending each shot you make?"

"It's the worst," he groaned. "Nothing quite like a shooting to make everybody want quadrupled paperwork, documenting every damn incident. Don't think you'll get away without having to give a full statement either."

She looked over at Gideon, who laughed and added,

"Tristan's right. I can promise you that as soon as Jasper's done at the hospital, everybody and their dog will be coming to get statements from you guys."

"*Great*," she muttered. "The least we can do is get moved home first."

"Oh, I like the sound of that," Gideon said, as he grasped her hand in his. "Home it is."

"Oh, *great*," Tristan muttered, beside them. "You guys won't get all *sucky-faced* and moronic over this, will you?"

"Absolutely," she stated. "It's the least we can do to let you know how serious we are about starting over."

Tristan groaned. and they burst out laughing, keeping up the teasing all the way to her house.

This concludes Book 3 of Man Down: Gideon.

Read about Tristan: Man Down, Book 4

Man Down:
Tristan
(Book #4)

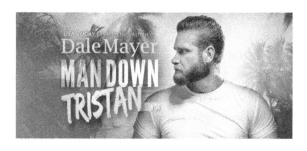

There is no greater motive than bloodlust, DNA, and revenge mixed up in a cocktail of hatred ...

Tristan had volunteered his assistance on Mason's case, as Jasper needs men he can count on. Tristan wasn't expecting to meet the very interesting new coroner, but, as the bodies pile up and the mystery deepens, Tristan appreciates her expertise ... and the spark between them.

Amarylis had no idea working on Coronado base would be so interesting ... or so dangerous. Apparently someone watched her during her work at the scene of a shooting, noting she had picked up something which someone wanted ... badly.

Now in danger and caught up in Tristan's case, Amarylis can only hope he gets to the bottom of this mess, before she ends up on her own table in the morgue ...

T RISTAN MONTGOMERY SAT up stiffly. He hadn't let on that the blow to the head he'd taken two days ago had resulted in a stiff neck and some shoulder injury. He would talk to Pearl about giving him some physical therapy, hoping that she would just wring him out a couple times, instead of making him go to the doctor. Tristan wasn't all that into doctors these days, especially not in hospitals.

They'd spent all day yesterday completing their statements and cleaning up the red tape mess from the shooting in the ER. It was a good shoot, absolutely no argument about that, but just enough was going on right now that everybody had to make sure the paperwork was dealt with appropriately. Tristan was in the second spare room in Gideon's house, and he walked downstairs slowly.

Pearl took one look at him and ordered, "Sit."

He immediately sat, and she came up behind him and started working his muscles. He groaned with joy, as, one by one, the knots released, and the pain eased up.

"Now go have a hot shower, and, when you come back downstairs again," she said, "there'll be coffee."

He smiled. "How come there aren't two of you?"

"Because one of her is enough to handle," Gideon declared from the kitchen, where he was busy cooking. "And, if you want pancakes, get your ass back down here fast."

"On it, boss." He quickly raced upstairs, feeling so much looser and better after the massage. Pearl had worked his muscles over good, and it made all the difference. After a quick shower, with the heat soaking into his sore muscles, he was soon downstairs and ready for breakfast. When he sat down, Pearl set a plateful of pancakes in front of him. Tristan said, "You don't have to feel guilty and give me preferential treatment for having saved your life. Gideon and

Jasper were both at the ready."

"I know that," she replied cheerfully, "but it makes me happy."

"In that case, fly at it," Tristan murmured, around a mouthful of pancakes.

She chuckled, as she sat down, and asked, "Who was that nurse, by the way?" He looked over at her blankly. "The nurse who was giving you a hard time at the hospital."

He shrugged. "I don't know. Seems like everybody gives me a hard time these days."

"She was cute."

He narrowed his gaze at her. "Oh no, you don't."

"Oh no, I don't, *what?*" she asked, an innocent expression on her face.

"No matchmaking."

"I don't have to matchmake, and she looked positively delighted that I was there, yelling at you."

He snorted. "Yeah, why would someone like to hear someone else getting yelled at?"

"Maybe they're just getting a word in, without being interrupted."

The teasing soon stopped as the three of them dug into their breakfasts when Tristan asked, "What about Jasper? Anybody hear from him this morning? He was supposed to call with an update."

"Not yet," Gideon replied. "I suspect he'll be here anytime now. He has a way of showing up when the pancakes are done."

"In that case, we should save him some," Pearl suggested.

Tristan shook his head. "No, we're not saving him anything."

But the door opened without warning, and Jasper stepped inside, sniffing the air. He entered the kitchen and looked at the leftovers on the table and grabbed a plate and sat down. "Jeez," he muttered. "You could have at least told me breakfast was ready."

"Ha," Gideon said. "I figured you would be here anyway."

As soon as he got a couple bites in, Tristan looked over at Jasper and asked, "So, what's going on?"

Jasper sighed. "Well, first off, a nurse at the hospital wants to know how you got released without a doctor's permission and if you're okay. She's feeling quite concerned because she heard what happened." Jasper gave Tristan a big grin. "You better give her a call."

Tristan flushed. "I'll pass. Next?"

"Other than that, we got all the paperwork filed on the hospital shooting. It's been reviewed, and you're in the clear. You're also back to active duty, as long as you feel well enough," he added, critically assessing him.

"Of course I am," Tristan stated, glaring at him. "I barely got hurt."

"*Right*," Pearl noted. "That's why all your muscles were locked up when you came down this morning, especially your neck and your shoulders."

He stared in disbelief. "I can't believe you threw me under the bus."

"When it comes to matters of life and death, or pain and health, I'll do it every time. You can count on that," she declared.

"Yeah, I do like that about you." Tristan smiled, then looked over at Jasper. "So, where do we stand?"

Jasper gave him a fat smile. "I brought over some very

interesting details. So, gather around, and let's get a start on this. Maybe, if we're lucky, we can nail this down and find out who is behind all this, starting with the shooting of Mason."

"I sure as hell wish we knew whether it was a good shot or a bad shot," Gideon noted, looking over at Jasper.

"That's another good point," Jasper replied, "and we aren't likely to know that, not until we get to the end of this."

"I don't understand," Pearl said, not making heads or tails of it. "What do you mean about a good shot or a bad shot?"

Tristan explained, "In this case, a *bad shot* means Drew was aiming to kill Mason but missed his kill shot a bit and just wounded Mason instead. A *good shot* means Drew aimed to wound Mason and hoped to get away with this, free and clear."

"But Drew didn't get away, did he?" she asked.

Tristan nodded. "No, which is why I'll say it was a bad shot, and Drew was killed over it."

"You guys play for keeps, don't you?" Pearl asked.

"No, we don't, but these guys do," Jasper replied, with a nod. "And, therefore, somebody has to play the game the same way the bad guys do. Don't worry, Pearl," he added. "We're getting a hell of a lot further down the path. We know a lot more than we did before, so we will get this stopped."

"If you say so," she grumbled, with a headshake.

Tristan smacked her hand lightly. "We've got this. Don't you worry. You'll be safe now, and, with any luck, so will Mason and Tesla and Sebastian and Nicholas and Elizabeth." Tristan eyed the last pancake on the table, glanced at the others, decided not to ask, and snagged it right up. "I am the injured one, after all."

Pearl laughed, while Gideon just narrowed his gaze at the empty platter.

Jasper added, "Better eat up, Tristan, because you're next at bat."

Find Book 4 here!

To find out more visit Dale Mayer's website.

https://geni.us/DMSMDTristan

Author's Note

Thank you for reading Gideon: Man Down, Book 3! If you enjoyed the book, please take a moment and leave a short review.

Dear reader,

I love to hear from readers, and you can contact me at my website: www.dalemayer.com or at my Facebook author page. To be informed of new releases and special offers, sign up for my newsletter or follow me on BookBub. And if you are interested in joining Dale Mayer's Reader Group, here is the Facebook sign up page.
http://geni.us/DaleMayerFBGroup

Cheers,
Dale Mayer

About the Author

Dale Mayer is a *USA Today* best-selling author, best known for her SEALs military romances, her Psychic Visions series, and her Lovely Lethal Garden cozy series. Her contemporary romances are raw and full of passion and emotion (Broken But ... Mending, Hathaway House series). Her thrillers will keep you guessing (Kate Morgan, By Death series), and her romantic comedies will keep you giggling (*It's a Dog's Life*, a stand-alone novella; and the Broken Protocols series, starring Charming Marvin, the cat).

Dale honors the stories that come to her—and some of them are crazy, break all the rules and cross multiple genres!

To go with her fiction, she also writes nonfiction in many different fields, with books available on résumé writing, companion gardening, and the US mortgage system. All her books are available in print and ebook format.

Connect with Dale Mayer Online

Dale's Website – www.dalemayer.com
Twitter – @DaleMayer
Facebook Page – geni.us/DaleMayerFBFanPage
Facebook Group – geni.us/DaleMayerFBGroup
BookBub – geni.us/DaleMayerBookbub
Instagram – geni.us/DaleMayerInstagram
Goodreads – geni.us/DaleMayerGoodreads
Newsletter – geni.us/DaleNews

Printed in the USA
CPSIA information can be obtained
at www.ICGtesting.com
LVHW021621191024
794252LV00011B/106